A Book of Blessings
for
CNI Pastors and Lay Leaders

A Book of Blessings
for
CNI Pastors and Lay Leaders

Prepared by
Revd Fr Monodeep Daniel BAC

THE CHURCH OF NORTH INDIA SYNOD
2011

A Book of Blessings for CNI Pastors and Lay Leaders – published by the Rev. Dr. Ashish Amos of the Indian Society for Promoting Christian Knowledge (ISPCK), Post Box 1585, 1654, Madarsa Road, Kashmere Gate, Delhi-110006, for The Church of North India Synod, CNI Bhavan, 16 Pandit Pant Marg, Delhi-110001.

ISBN: 978-81-8465-184-3

Laser typeset at **ISPCK,** Post Box 1585, 1654, Madarsa Road, Kashmere Gate, Delhi-110006.
Tel: 23866323, Fax: 91-11-23865490
e-mail: ashish@ispck.org.in • ella@ispck.org.in
website: www.ispck.org.in

Contents

A

D

E

F

M

N

O

P

Q

R

S

T

U

V

Foreword

Blessings are more than mere words. The words we speak, whether blessings or anything else, can make the difference in our life and in the lives of those around us. In the Old Testament book of Genesis there is a story that illustrates this very clearly. In chapter 27 we find the story of Jacob taking the "blessing" that had been reserved for his older brother Esau. Isaac, their father, planned to give the "blessing" to Esau. Rebecca, the mother of Jacob and Esau loved Jacob more and plotted with Jacob to trick Isaac into giving the "blessing" to Jacob rather than Esau. It is interesting that all this scheming took place over a few sentences to be spoken by Isaac.

Most often we don't realize how powerful the words we speak are, whether we are speaking to someone else or about them. There is great power in praying a blessing over others. We, as a society and as Christians in this society, need to learn this truth: the words we speak are more than words.

Blessings, as sacramental, are used to confer special sacredness or grace to both animate and inanimate things. Therefore blessings can be applied to such objects as water, medals, candles, and scapulars. This is so because the blessings of these objects act as reminders to us of certain truths of our faith. For example, water takes on a new meaning after a blessing. It becomes a resemblance of eternal life and helps us remember our baptism. When blessed candles not only supply light but become constant reminders of the Eternal Light and our responsibility to that Light. Therefore, we must learn to speak words of blessing into the lives of others: friends, neighbors, our nation, our leaders, our world and our things etc.

This Book of Blessings is a first of its kind for the congregations of Church of North India and I must appreciate the efforts of our Commission on Liturgy and congratulate its members, particularly Fr. Monodeep Daniel and Rt. Rev. Vijay B. Sathe for bringing it out in the shape of a book. I hope that this book will broaden our horizon of understanding the importance of blessings to the listed as they come to us as blessings.

May God bless us and help us bless others!

The Most Rev. Dr. Purely Lyngdoh
Moderator
Church of North India Synod

Preface

U nder the mandate of the Synod Liturgical Commission we took up the task of preparing a book of blessing for pastors. This need was brought to our notice by the members of our Commission in our first meeting and it took almost three years of work to compile this volume. While most of the drafting was done by Fr Monodeep Daniel, the Commission members did the editorial work. I want specifically to acknowledge the contribution of Revd (Adv.) Deodatta Kasote, Revd Binoy K. Topno, Revd David Roy and Revd Samuel Halder whose unfailing attendance at our meetings and working through the drafts of this book with suggestions was very helpful.

The prayers for various blessings will be useful for the pastors to help people understand the value of our things and abilities that God gives us. It is also a way to offer these to God. The use of traditional customs of blessing the water is also offered, but keeping in view the variety of practices in diverse regions in the *Church of North India* we have kept it altogether optional. The prayers of blessings can be used with responses or without it, similarly the use of blessed water as a sign is optional. We suggest that the resources of prayers, scripture readings and symbolic actions be employed or adopted by the Minister or presbyter as best suited for the occasion or place.

With each blessing a reading of a Psalm is also suggested. This also is only a suggestion and some other appropriate scripture text could be used by the Minister.

With these words of introduction I offer this book for the glory of God and the good of His people. My prayer is that may these prayers help our people to be good stewards of all that God has given us by blessing them and setting them apart for God's use in the work of His salvation.

'In your presence O Lord, is the fullness of joy'.

The Rt. Revd. Vijay B Sathe
Chairperson: Synod Liturgical Commission

Introductory Notes

Spirituality aims to restore the image of God within each person. This image of God has been spoiled due to our compulsive behaviour to rebel against God our creator. In other words we have lost that divine life and power within us that shaped God's image within our being. Indeed, the incorrigible extreme of our behaviour brings sorrow and suffering to our fellow human-beings and other creatures too. In spite of our behaviour, God comes to us with love. He came to us in Jesus, his beloved and only begotten Son, and reconciled us to himself.

In the death of Jesus two things were exposed: the extreme of our wickedness on one hand and the extent of divine love on the other. Similarly in the resurrection of Jesus two things were offered to us: one was life over death and the other was power over evil. This offer of life and power is God's gift to us if we repent of our wickedness and accept the offer of life and power that God freely gives to us in the Lord Jesus Christ. This is God's unconditional favour to us which we do not deserve or merit. Now we know that our Lord Jesus has ascended to be with the heavenly Father, but he sent the Holy Spirit to offer His gift of life and power which we saw in the life, death and resurrection of the Lord Jesus Christ.

Of this divine favour, which we do not deserve, God gives us plenty of signs. One among these is our privilege to 'bless'. By blessing we ask God to 'sanctify' because it is by His divine will that we have been sanctified (Heb 10.10). Sanctification means to make things 'holy'. It means that God sets things and people apart for his use. By their use God reaches out to all people with His love. The things may be our resources and our abilities. To bless is an act of faith. We believe that God honours our faith and our intentions. In response He 'sanctifies' what we 'bless'. As a sign we can use the mixed symbol of water-and-salt to bless. What we bless, the Holy Spirit sanctifies. Sanctification is purely God's gift.

Section-1 is prayer for the *Blessing of Water*, which makes it a sign to bless other things. Only the Presbyter/Bishop has the privilege to bless the water.

Section-2 is a schedule of *Various Blessing*. These blessing are for people, things, functions and our abilities. A Minister can use *Various Blessings* of Section-2 without sprinkling the blessed water.

The *Various Blessing* can be used by any church elder or licensed Minister or a respected church member in good-standing. This is so because in the CNI we believe in the priesthood of all believers (CNI Constitution Part-1).

Fr. Monodeep Daniel BAC
Secretary: Synod Liturgical Commission

Section - 1

Blessing of the Water

It has been an old custom to sprinkle Holy Water on objects and people to confirm their sanctification by the Holy Spirit.

The Water should be blessed using the following form of prayer:

Presbyter   Our help is in the name of the Lord.

All   **Who has made heaven and earth.**

Presbyter   Let us remember that the Lord Jesus Christ said "Let anyone who is thirsty come to me, and let the one who believes in me drink, for the Scripture says, *Out of the believer's heart shall flow rivers of living water*". Let us therefore thank the Lord for the gift of water.

Thanksgiving for the Gift of Water

Presbyter   Lord Our God we thank you for creating water to give us life and wholeness, to refresh us and rejuvenate us.

All   **Blessed be God.**

Presbyter   We thank you gracious God that, when floods threatened the survival of the human race and brought to people the sense of their sins, you pardoned their iniquities and promised that floods should destroy the earth no more. The rainbow in the clouds is the sign of your beauty and favour.

All   **Blessed be God.**

Presbyter	We thank you O God our saviour that you led your people through the Red Sea liberating them from the bondage of Pharaoh and saving them from the hands of his army till they reached the land of freedom.
All	**Blessed be God.**

Presbyter	In the fullness of time God sent his servant John whose baptism of repentance prepared the people for the kingdom of God and for the baptism of the Holy Spirit through Jesus Christ our Lord.
All	**Blessed be God.**

Presbyter	Lord Jesus passed through the waters of death, but God raised him from the dead and opened to us the gates of eternal life.
All	**Blessed be God.**

Presbyter	In ancient times God promised to pour out his Spirit upon all people. Led by his Holy Spirit we now turn to God and call him Father. He gives us new birth and leads us from untruth to truth, from darkness to light, from death to eternal live.
All	**Blessed be God.**

Presbyter	So whenever we are sprinkled when blessing ourselves we thank God for his gift to us of new life in Baptism. Let us now bless this water with salt.

The Presbyter shall bless the salt as following:

Almighty God, the creator and sustainer of all things, through your mercy we have this salt to celebrate your bounty; hear our prayer and bless this salt which you have made for our use; grant that it may preserve all that is good, and give health and cleansing to all on which it is sprinkled and protect your people from the assault of the evil one, through Jesus Christ our Lord. Amen.

The Presbyter shall then bless the water as following:

> O Lord our God, you created this world out of chaos and placed limits to the waters, you spared Noah and his family along with animals on the waters, you parted the Red sea for your people to walk on dry shores, and made water the sign of our new birth at Baptism; hear our prayer to pour your blessing on this water that it may mark the power of your presence to sanctify us and things for our use. Grant that all who call on your name and are sprinkled with this water may be healed and defended from the hurt of the assault of the evil one, through Jesus Christ our Lord. Amen

The Presbyter shall then mix the salt in the water and say the following prayer:

> O Lord God, the Sovereign ruler of this universe, for us you overcame the powers of wickedness and death through the resurrection of your Son our Lord Jesus Christ; bless this mixture of salt and water so that wherever it is sprinkled your people may be healed and delivered always welcoming the saints and rejoicing in the blessed peace of your Holy Spirit through Jesus Christ our Lord. Amen

Presbyter: Let us praise the Lord

All   **The Lord's name be praised**

Presbyter   As our saviour Christ has taught us let us pray

All   **Our Father in heaven, hallowed by your name, your kingdom come, your will be done on earth as in heaven. Give us today our daily bread. Forgive us our sins as we forgive those who sin against us. Do not bring us to the time of trial but deliver us from evil. For the kingdom, the power and the glory are yours now and forever. Amen.**

This holy water can be prepared and kept in a clean jar for blessing (by Bishops, Presbyters, Deacons and Lay Leaders/Readers holding Bishop's license). If a sprinkler is not available the Minister can keep the holy water in a cup and sprinkle with fresh leaves preferably of Neem, Mango and any suitable tree or flower to symbolise wholeness and cleansing.

Words of Grace

Can be said by Deacons, or licensed Lay Leaders/Readers or any elder.

**The Grace of our Lord Jesus Christ and the
love of God and the fellowship of the Holy Spirit
be with us all now and always. Amen.**

Words of Blessing

*Also called the Aronic blessing which should be
said by Presbyters and Bishops.*

**Unto God's gracious mercy and protection we commit you. The
Lord bless you, and keep you:
the Lord make his face to shine upon you,
and be gracious to you: the Lord lift up
his countenance upon you, and give**

**you peace, and the blessing of God Almighty,
the Father, the Son and the
Holy Spirit be among you and
with you all now and always.**

Amen.

Section - 2

Various Blessings

A

1. *Acolytes*

Minister: Our help is in the name of the Lord.

People: **Who has made heaven and earth.**

The Holy Water may be sprinkled to bless the acolytes ready with their candles in procession.

Reading: Psalm 27

O Lord our God, you created light to dispel chaos and darkness; your Son Jesus said *I am the light of the world*; bless these candles and those who carry them to remind us to shine out as light exposing and expelling the darkness of wickedness and oppression of this world, and glorify you as the Lord and creator of this universe; through Jesus Christ our Lord who live and reigns with you and the Holy Spirit one God now and forever. **Amen**.

Minister: Let us praise the Lord

People: **The Lord's name be praised**

Minister: As our saviour Christ has taught us so we pray

All: **Our Father in heaven... .**

The Minister may end with the words of grace or if a presbyter is present with benediction.

2. *Actors*

Minister: Our help is in the name of the Lord.

People: **Who has made heaven and earth.**

The Holy Water may be sprinkled to bless the actors ready to stage a play/drama.

Reading: Psalm 78.1-7

O Lord God, the inspirer of people, you unfold the plan of our salvation through the actions of women and men in history; hear our prayer to bless these actors (now ready to act in the play to unfold the story of Christmas/Easter/_____) with alertness and stamina to bring out the message of the story through their skill of action and voice for the benefit of the people; this we ask in the name of Jesus Christ our Lord who lives and reigns with you and the Holy Spirit one God now and always. **Amen.**

Presbyter: Let us praise the Lord

People: **The Lord's name be praised**

Minister: As our saviour Christ has taught us so we pray

All: **Our Father in heaven... .**

The Minister may end with the words of grace or if a presbyter is present with benediction.

3. *Aircraft*

Minister: Our help is in the name of the Lord.

People: **Who has made heaven and earth.**

The Holy Water may be sprinkled in the aircraft to bless it.

Reading: Psalm 68.4-10

O Lord God of heavens, your cherubim move with swiftness across the heavens; hear our prayer to bless this aircraft that it may accomplish its purpose to transport people (or goods) through the passage of air in swiftness and safety; bless the pilots and crew with alertness, skills and wisdom to control its mechanisms efficiently; this we ask in the name of Jesus Christ our Lord who lives and reigns with you and the Holy Spirit one God now and always. **Amen.**

Presbyter: Let us praise the Lord

People: **The Lord's name be praised**

Minister: As our saviour Christ has taught us so we pray

All: **Our Father in heaven... .**

The Minister may end with the words of grace or if a presbyter is present with benediction.

4. *Airport*

Minister: Our help is in the name of the Lord.

People: **Who has made heaven and earth.**

The Holy Water may be sprinkled in the main lounge or some area of the building to bless it.

Reading: Psalm 67.

O Lord our God, the King of this universe, you found a station in the humble manger in Bethlehem for your Son; hear our prayer to bless this airport and all its workers that they may efficiently serve the needs of all passengers who arrive and depart from here to their various destinations; endow them with skill to use the various instruments with which this airport is equipped so that this place is safe from harm and from accidents, this we ask in the name of Jesus Christ our Lord who lives and reigns with you and the Holy Spirit one God now and always. **Amen.**

Minister:	Let us praise the Lord
People:	The Lord's name be praised

Minister:	As our saviour Christ has taught us so we pray
All:	**Our Father in heaven... .**

The Minister may end with the words of grace or if a presbyter is present with benediction.

5.   *Ambulance*

Minister:	Our help is in the name of the Lord.
People:	**Who has made heaven and earth.**

The Holy Water may be sprinkled in the ambulance to bless it.

Reading: Psalm 121.

O Lord our God, the healer of our wounds and diseases, your Son Jesus Christ brought wholeness to the sick who were brought to him, hear our prayer to bless this ambulance which we now set apart to transport the sick and the wounded to the hospital so that they may be relieved from their trauma; this we ask in the name of Jesus Christ our Lord who lives and reigns with you and the Holy Spirit one God now and always. **Amen**.

Minister:	Let us praise the Lord
People:	**The Lord's name be praised**

Minister:	As our saviour Christ has taught us so we pray
All:	**Our Father in heaven... .**

The Minister may end with the words of grace or if a presbyter is present with benediction.

6. *Animals in the wild/sanctuary*

Minister: Our help is in the name of the Lord.

People: Who has made heaven and earth.

Holy Water may be sprinkled in that area of a national park.

Reading: Psalm 104.1-30

O Lord God, you made us for yourself and sustain us through your word, you created the animals to inhabit the world where your Son our Lord Jesus Christ also lived with them for forty days in the wilderness, hear our prayer and bless all the animals of this sanctuary that they may grow in abundance and enrich life on this planet; may our world be free of hunters as we look forward to your new creation where all animals will live in harmony, this we ask in the name of Jesus Christ our Lord who lives and reigns with you and the Holy Spirit one God now and always. **Amen.**

Minister: Let us praise the Lord

People: The Lord's name be praised

Minister: As our saviour Christ has taught us so we pray

All: Our Father in heaven... .

The Minister may end with the words of grace or if a presbyter is present with benediction.

7. *Anniversary (Wedding)*

Minister: Our help is in the name of the Lord.

People: Who has made heaven and earth.

The Holy Water may be sprinkled on the couple to bless them.

Reading: Psalm 100 or if appropriate 128

O Lord our God, your Son Jesus with his mother and his family, brought joy to the wedding at Cana and blessed many children;

hear our prayer and bless, **A** and **B** , that loving one another they may continue in your love; bless, protect and guide them, pour out the riches of your grace on them that they love together in your peace and finally by your mercy obtain everlasting life. **Amen**

Minister:	Let us praise the Lord
People:	**The Lord's name be praised**

Minister:	As our saviour Christ has taught us so we pray
All:	**Our Father in heaven... .**

The Minister may end with the words of grace or if a presbyter is present with benediction.

8.   *Art*

Minister:	Our help is in the name of the Lord.
People:	**Who has made heaven and earth.**

Care should be taken not to sprinkle the holy water on the piece of art but in the area around it.

Reading: Psalm 96

O glorious God, enthroned in the beauty of holiness, you have made us like yourself to create beauty, hear our prayer to bless this work of art expressing human heart and mind so that it may enrich our culture, deepen our emotions and beautify our surroundings; bless _____ (*artist's name*) with greater measure of skills, creativity and imagination so that he/she may continue to contribute to the enrichment of society; this we ask in the name of Jesus Christ our Lord who lives and reigns with you and the Holy Spirit one God now and always. **Amen**.

Minister:	Let us praise the Lord
People:	**The Lord's name be praised**

Minister: As our saviour Christ has taught us so we pray

All: **Our Father in heaven... .**

The Minister may end with the words of grace or if a presbyter is present with benediction.

9.   *Ash*

Minister: Our help is in the name of the Lord.

People: **Who has made heaven and earth.**

Reading: Psalm 130

Almighty and eternal God, we return to dust and ash, yet you do not desire the death of any sinner but forgive those who are penitent; bless this ash of palm leaves to remind us of our sins and morality and also of your promise to give us new and contrite hearts, so that sorrowing for our sins were may receive from you pardon and peace; through Jesus Christ our Lord who lives and reigns with you and the Holy Spirit one God, now and forever. **Amen.**

Minister: Let us praise the Lord

People: **The Lord's name be praised**

Minister: As our saviour Christ has taught us so we pray

All: **Our Father in heaven... .**

The Minister may end with the words of grace or if a presbyter is present with benediction.

10.   *Ashram*

Minister: Our help is in the name of the Lord.

People: **Who has made heaven and earth.**

The Holy Water may be sprinkled to bless those assembled.

Reading: Psalm 23

Eternal and invisible God, you are the truth of all that is seen and unseen to us. In your mercy you gave us the desire to feel you and find you in the stillness of our heart; bless O Lord and sanctify this Ashram that in its quietness we may know your presence and find your peace which is beyond all understanding; through Jesus Christ our Lord who lives and reign with you and the Holy Spirit one God now and always. Amen.

Minister:	Let us praise the Lord
People:	**The Lord's name be praised**

Minister:	As our saviour Christ has taught us so we pray
All:	**Our Father in Heaven... .**

The Minister may end with the words of grace or a presbyter by benediction.

11. *Assembly*

Minister:	Our help is in the name of the Lord.
People:	**Who has made heaven and earth.**

The Holy Water may be sprinkled to bless those assembled.

Reading: Psalm 1.

Eternal and glorious God, before you the assembly of Saints and angels swell their voices singling alleluia eternally; hear our prayer to bless this assembly (gathered here for the purpose of _____) that their deliberations may be meaningful and that they would glorify your name by doing all that is just and right, bless them with clarity of thought, harmony of purpose and discipline in proceedings, this we ask in the name of Jesus Christ our Lord who lives and reigns with you and the Holy Spirit one God now and always. **Amen.**

Minister:	Let us praise the Lord
People:	**The Lord's name be praised**

Minister:	As our saviour Christ has taught us so we pray
All:	**Our Father in Heaven... .**

The Minister may end with the words of grace or a presbyter by benediction.

12.   *Auditorium*

Minister:	Our help is in the name of the Lord.
People:	**Who has made heaven and earth.**

The Holy Water may be sprinkled to bless the Auditorium.

Reading: Psalm 82

O Lord our God, the great architect of this universe, you have given us your wisdom to design and to build with purpose, hear our prayer and bless this auditorium built for the purpose of gatherings of people that through their celebrations, deliberations, discussions or any other event your people may be built up in their capacities to serve others, through Jesus Christ our Lord who lives and reigns with you and the Holy Spirit one God now and forever. **Amen**

Minister:	Let us praise the Lord
People:	**The Lord's name be praised.**

Minister:	As our saviour Christ has taught us so we pray
All:	**Our Father in heaven... .**

The Minister may end with the words of grace or if a presbyter is present with benediction.

B

13. *Baby*

Minister:	Our help is in the name of the Lord.
People:	**Who has made heaven and earth.**

The Holy Water may be sprinkled on the baby to bless him/her.

Reading: Psalm 127

O Lord God, you delight us with the gift of life; hear our prayer and bless this baby to grow in wisdom and knowledge, in strength and vigour into a wholesome person, and may continually delight us with love and joy, through Jesus Christ our Lord who lives and reigns with you and the Holy Spirit one God now and forever. **Amen**

Minister:	Let us praise the Lord
People:	**The Lord's name be praised**

Minister:	As our saviour Christ has taught us so we pray
All:	**Our Father in heaven... .**

The Minister may end with the words of grace or if a presbyter is present with benediction.

14. *Bathroom*

Minister:	Our help is in the name of the Lord.
People:	**Who has made heaven and earth.**

The Holy Water may be sprinkled in the Bathroom to bless it.

Reading: Psalm 51.1-2

O Lord God, through your mercy we have water to revive ourselves, bless this bathroom so that all who use it may wash away filth and be refreshed; in our daily ablutions, O Lord, help us to stand before you with clean hands and pure hearts and minds through Jesus Christ our Lord who lives and reigns with you and the Holy Spirit one God now and forever. **Amen**

Minister:	Let us praise the Lord
People:	**The Lord's name be praised**

Minister:	As our saviour Christ has taught us so we pray
All:	**Our Father in heaven... .**

The Minister may end with the words of grace or a presbyter with benediction.

15. *Bedroom*

Minister:	Our help is in the name of the Lord.
People:	**Who has made heaven and earth.**

The Holy Water may be sprinkled on the Bed to bless it.

Reading: Psalm 116.1-7

O Lord our God, in your mercy we lie down in peace and sleep, for you alone make us dwell in safety; hear our prayer and bless this bedroom; guard it with your unfailing watchfulness all who take their rest here, that refreshed by the gift of sleep, they may serve you joyfully day by day, through Jesus Christ our Lord who lives and reigns with you and the Holy Spirit one God now and always. **Amen**.

Minister:	Let us praise the Lord
People:	**The Lord's name be praised**

Minister:	As our saviour Christ has taught us so we **pray**
All:	**Our Father in heaven... .**

The Minister may end with the words of grace or if a presbyter is present with benediction.

16.   *Bell for a Church*

Minister: Our help is in the name of the Lord.

People: Who has made heaven and earth.

The Holy Water may be sprinkled on the bell to bless it.

Reading: Psalm 115

O Lord our God, you endowed your people with skill to make good things; hear our prayer as we set apart this bell for your service; sanctify and hallow it that it's sound may inspire those who hear it to gather for praise and worship in your House to the glory of your name; through Jesus Christ our Lord who lives and reigns with you and the Holy Spirit one God now and forever. **Amen**

Minister: Let us praise the Lord

People: The Lord's name be praised

Minister: As our saviour Christ has taught us so we **pray**

All: Our Father in heaven... .

The Minister may end with the words of grace or if a presbyter is present with benediction.

17.   *Bench (for Garden, hall etc)*

Minister: Our help is in the name of the Lord.

People: Who has made heaven and earth.

The Holy Water may be sprinkled to bless the object.

Reading: Psalm 113

O Lord our God, our creator and redeemer, you created Garden of Eden for Adam and Eve to live and to take care of; bless O Lord this bench for people to sit and enjoy the beauty of this garden, refresh themselves and to praise your name as we, with the whole nature look forwards to that day when you will redeemed your creation from the pangs of destruction and death; through Jesus Christ our Lord who lives and reigns with you and the Holy Spirit one God now and always. **Amen**.

Minister:	Let us praise the Lord
People:	**The Lord's name be praised**

Minister:	As our saviour Christ has taught us so we **pray**
All:	**Our Father in heaven... .**

The Minister may end with the words of grace or if a presbyter is present with benediction.

18.   *Bible-study Group*

Minister:	Our help is in the name of the Lord.
People:	**Who has made heaven and earth.**

The Holy Water may be sprinkled to bless the members of the Bible Study group

Reading: Psalm 119.1-20

O Lord our God, the inspirer of prophets, apostles, evangelists and all other writers of the bible; your Son our Lord Jesus Christ expounded the sacred scriptures in the synagogue at Nazareth; hear our prayer to bless this Bible-Study group as that through their regular study of your word they may be nourished in faith and enable others to gain strength from it too, through Jesus Christ our Lord who lives and reigns with you and the Holy Spirit one God now and forever. **Amen**

Minister:	Let us praise the Lord
People:	**The Lord's name be praised**

Minister:	As our saviour Christ has taught us so we pray
All:	**Our Father in heaven... .**

The Minister may end with the words of grace or if a presbyter is present with benediction.

19.   *Bicycle*

Minister:	Our help is in the name of the Lord.
People:	**Who has made heaven and earth.**

The Holy Water may be sprinkled to bless the bicycle.

Reading: Psalm 113

O Lord our God, you gave us the desire and the strength to travel and to procure what we need; hear our prayer and bless this bicycle that it may carry those who use it to safely reach their destinations; through Jesus Christ our Lord who lives and reigns with you and the Holy Spirit one God now and forever. **Amen**

Minister:	Let us praise the Lord
People:	**The Lord's name be praised**

Minister:	As our saviour Christ has taught us so we pray
All:	**Our Father in heaven... .**

The Minister may end with the words of grace or if a presbyter is present with benediction.

20.   *Birthday*

Minister:	Our help is in the name of the Lord.
People:	**Who has made heaven and earth.**

The Holy Water may be sprinkled to bless the one whose Birthday is being celebrated.

Reading: Psalm 67

Gracious and loving Lord, in your mercy you give us life and health year by year; hear our prayer and bless _____(*name*) whose birthday we are celebrating. Bless *her/him* with health and wholeness, bless *him/her* abundance of joy of knowing you, loving you and serving you more and more in the coming days of *her/his* life; through Jesus Christ our Lord who lives and reigns with you and the Holy Spirit one God now and forever. **Amen**

Minister: Let us praise the Lord

People: **The Lord's name be praised**

Minister: As our saviour Christ has taught us so we pray

All: **Our Father in heaven... .**

The Minister may end with the words of grace or if a presbyter is present with benediction.

21.   *Birds*

Minister: Our help is in the name of the Lord.

People: **Who has made heaven and earth.**

(NOTE: This prayer should not be misused for birds kept in cage)

Reading: Psalm 104.1-13

O Lord God, the creator of this world, you made the birds to nest in the trees and fly in air across the world; hear our prayer and bless these birds that their sight and sound may ever fill our hearts with delight, bless that they may they always be free to fly and our world be made free from the snare of the fowlers, through Jesus Christ our Lord who lives and reigns with you and the Holy Spirit one God now and forever. **Amen**

Minister: Let us praise the Lord

People: **The Lord's name be praised**

Minister: As our saviour Christ has taught us so we pray

All: **Our Father in heaven... .**

The Minister may end with the words of grace or if a presbyter is present with benediction.

22.   *Boat*

Minister: Our help is in the name of the Lord.

People: Who has made heaven and earth.

The Holy Water may be sprinkled in the boat to bless it.

Reading: Psalm 29

O Lord God, your voice far more powerful than the might of the waters that thunders over the vast oceans; your Son our Lord Jesus Christ saved the boat and people from perishing in the stormy sea; hear our prayer to bless this boat and all those who use it so that in their skilful hands it may transport in safety people and goods through the passage of waters, through Jesus Christ our Lord who lives and reigns with you and the Holy Spirit one God now and forever. **Amen**

Minister: Let us praise the Lord

People: The Lord's name be praised

Minister: As our saviour Christ has taught us so we pray

All: Our Father in heaven... .

The Minister may end with the words of grace or if a presbyter is present with benediction.

23.   *Book(s)*

Minister: Our help is in the name of the Lord.

People: Who has made heaven and earth.

Caution may be observed not to sprinkle excessive amount of Holy Water on the books.

Reading: Psalm 119.1-8

Blessed are you, Lord God, the fountain of all knowledge, you desire learning to flourish; hear our prayer to bless this book/ *these books* so that those who read it may benefit for its contents and bless them to be empowered with understanding, through Jesus Christ our Lord who lives and reigns with you and the Holy Spirit one God now and forever. **Amen**

Minister: Let us praise the Lord

People: The Lord's name be praised

Minister: As our saviour Christ has taught us so we pray

All: Our Father in heaven... .

The Minister may end with the words of grace or if a presbyter is present with benediction.

24.   *Bridge*

Minister: Our help is in the name of the Lord.

People: Who has made heaven and earth.

The Holy Water may be sprinkled to bless the bridge.

Reading: Psalm 46

O Lord God, even the Red sea could not stop your people to cross over to the other shore; hear our prayer to bless this bridge so that people would safely cross over to the other side to accomplish their duties and tasks which they have undertaken. Bless it to be sturdy and strong to withstand tempests and storms for years to come; through Jesus Christ our Lord who lives and reigns with you and the Holy Spirit one God now and forever. **Amen**

Minister: Let us praise the Lord

People: The Lord's name be praised

Minister: As our saviour Christ has taught us so we pray

All: Our Father in heaven... .

The Minister may end with the words of grace or if a presbyter is present with benediction.

25. *Buildings*

Minister: Our help is in the name of the Lord.

People: Who has made heaven and earth.

The Holy Water may be sprinkled throughout the building to bless it.

Reading: Psalm 48

O Lord our God, you willed the people to build Jerusalem the glorious city with intelligence, skill and labour; hear our prayer and bless this building (and all those who have constructed it), and those who will live (or work) here. Bless it to be safe and strong that it may serve the purpose for which it has been built; through Jesus Christ our Lord who lives and reigns with you and the Holy Spirit one God now and forever. **Amen**

Minister: Let us praise the Lord

People: The Lord's name be praised

Minister: As our saviour Christ has taught us so we pray

All: Our Father in heaven... .

The Minister may end with the words of grace or if a presbyter is present with benediction.

26. *Bus*

Minister: Our help is in the name of the Lord.

People: Who has made heaven and earth.

The Holy Water may be sprinkled to bless the bus, its drivers, conductors and the maintenance staff.

Reading: Psalm 105.1-4

O Lord our God, you gave us the desire to reach to the far ends of this earth; hear our prayer and bless this bus that it may safely carry those who travel in it to their destinations; bless the drivers, conductors and the mechanical experts with alertness and stamina so that they may succeed in their endeavours to maintain and to drive this bus; through Jesus Christ our Lord who lives and reigns with you and the Holy Spirit one God now and forever. **Amen**

Minister: Let us praise the Lord

People: **The Lord's name be praised**

The Minister may end with the words of grace or a presbyter by benediction.

27.   *Business*

Minister: Our help is in the name of the Lord.

People: **Who has made heaven and earth.**

The Holy Water may be sprinkled on those undertaking a business.
Reading: Psalm 24.

O Lord God, governor of this world, your Son our Lord Jesus enhanced the business of the fishermen in Galilee by the miraculous catch of fish; hear our prayer and bless this business (of _____) undertaken to meet the demands of the people. May it excel in quality and adequately meet the demands of the market (both in India and abroad), may those undertaking this venture be endowed with wisdom and stamina to become accomplished their endeavour and succeed in their business; through Jesus Christ our Lord who lives and reigns with you and the Holy Spirit one God now and forever. **Amen**

Minister: Let us praise the Lord

People: **The Lord's name be praised**

Minister: As our saviour Christ has taught us so we pray

All: **Our Father in heaven... .**

The Minister may end with the words of grace or if a presbyter is present with benediction.

C

28.   *Cake*

Minister:	Our help is in the name of the Lord.
People:	**Who has made heaven and earth.**

The Holy Water may be sprinkled on the cake with caution not to drench it.

Reading: Psalm 106.1-5.

O Lord our God, you fill our hearts and homes with joy of fellowship and kinship, your servant David joyfully received clusters of raisins and cakes of figs from Abigail; bless this cake O Lord to be for us a sign of unity and joy in the ceremony of cutting it and thereafter partaking of it. May the memory of these happy moment refresh us for many years to come; through Jesus Christ our Lord who lives and reigns with you and the Holy Spirit one God now and forever. **Amen**

Minister:	Let us praise the Lord
People:	**The Lord's name be praised**

Minister:	As our saviour Christ has taught us so we pray
All:	**Our Father in heaven... .**

The Minister may end with the words of grace or if a presbyter is present with benediction.

29.   *Car*

Minister:	Our help is in the name of the Lord.
People:	**Who has made heaven and earth.**

The Holy Water may be sprinkled on the car and its owners to bless.
Reading: Psalm 23

O Lord our God, your Son Jesus travelled to villages and towns in Galilee and the holy Apostles travelled to the ends of the world to proclaim the Good News of the Kingdom of Heaven; you give us desire to travel through this beautiful world that you have created; hear our prayer and bless this car and all those who travel in it, keep them safe from all accidents and mishaps, may this car accomplish the purpose for which it had been procured, keep it safe under your protection; through Jesus Christ our Lord who lives and reigns with you and the Holy Spirit one God now and forever. **Amen**

Minister: Let us praise the Lord

People: The Lord's name be praised

Minister: As our saviour Christ has taught us so we pray

All: Our Father in heaven... .

The Minister may end with the words of grace or if a presbyter is present with benediction.

30.   Cart

Minister: Our help is in the name of the Lord.

People: Who has made heaven and earth.

The Holy Water may be sprinkled on the cart and the animals (ox, cows, buffalos or horse that will pull it) to bless them.

Reading: Psalm 145

Lord our God, your people transported goods and material to build your glorious temple; hear our prayer and bless this cart so that it my securely transport goods from one place to another so that the needs of the people and requirements of industry may be met, through Jesus Christ our Lord who lives and reigns with you and the Holy Spirit one God now and forever. **Amen**

Minister: Let us praise the Lord

People: The Lord's name be praised

Minister: As our saviour Christ has taught us so we pray

All: Our Father in heaven... .

The Minister may end with the words of grace or if a presbyter is present with benediction.

31.   *Cemetery*

Minister: Our help is in the name of the Lord.

People: Who has made heaven and earth.

The Holy Water may be sprinkled on the gates of the cemetery and on its grounds, and on the people gathered for the occasion to bless them.

Reading: Psalm 90

Lord our God, you are the giver of life and do not desire any one to perish; your servant Lazarus was laid in a tomb and was resuscitated by your Son our Lord Jesus to life; hear our prayer and bless this cemetery where faithful souls lie so that just as we believe that they rest in peace in paradise, may our faith in their resurrection be ever strengthened, through Jesus Christ our Lord the conqueror of death, who lives and reigns with you and the Holy Spirit one God now and forever. **Amen**

Minister: Let us praise the Lord

People: The Lord's name be praised

Minister: As our saviour Christ has taught us so we pray

All: Our Father in heaven... .

The Minister may end with the words of grace or if a presbyter is present with benediction.

32.   *Centre (for Study, Research etc).*

Minister: Our help is in the name of the Lord.

People: Who has made heaven and earth.

The Holy Water may be sprinkled in the building.

Reading: Psalm 111

O Lord our God, you gave intelligence to your servant Apostle Paul not only to know the Hebrew Scripture but also the Greek poets to say 'For we too are his offspring'. You gave Evangelist Luke the aptitude to investigate and research and your Holy Spirit for writing the gospel; hear our prayer and bless this building (and all those who have constructed it), and those who will live (or work) here. Bless the researchers and scholars with inspiration, discipline, commitment, intelligence and aptitude to accomplish their research and articulate their finding by writing articles and books. Bless this building to be safe and strong that it may serve the purpose for which it has been built; through Jesus Christ our Lord who lives and reigns with you and the Holy Spirit one God now and forever. **Amen**

Minister:	Let us praise the Lord
People:	**The Lord's name be praised**

Minister:	As our saviour Christ has taught us so we pray
All:	**Our Father in heaven... .**

The Minister may end with the words of grace or if a presbyter is present with benediction.

33. *Chalice and Paten (Holy Vessels for the Lord's Supper)*

Minister:	Our help is in the name of the Lord.
People:	**Who has made heaven and earth.**

The Holy Water may be sprinkled on the vessels to sanctify them.

Reading: Psalm 138

Almighty and everlasting God, you had ordained under the old covenant that vessels should be set apart for the service of your sanctuary; hear our prayer to bless and hallow this chalice and paten which we bless in your name for the ministration of the *Eucharist* (or Thanksgiving) of your Son Jesus Christ who for our salvation offered himself a full and perfect sacrifice once and for all upon the cross and now is our great high priest, interceding for us before your mighty throne on high, where he lives and reigns with you and the Holy Spirit one God now and forever. **Amen**.

Minister: Let us praise the Lord

People: The Lord's name be praised

Minister: As our saviour Christ has taught us so we pray

All: Our Father in heaven... .

The Minister may end with the words of grace or if a presbyter is present with benediction.

34.   *Chapel*

Minister: Our help is in the name of the Lord.

People: Who has made heaven and earth.

The Holy Water may be sprinkled throughout the chapel, its vestry, its walls, floors and altar and the people to bless them.

Reading: Psalm 84

O Lord our God, you desire people to set apart places for your glory; hear our prayer and bless this chapel so that those associated with _____ (*name of the institution*) may use this place to offer you praise and worship, have a quiet atmosphere for meditation, find in here inspiration to work and consolation in distress, through Jesus Christ our Lord who lives and reigns with you and the Holy Spirit one God now and forever. **Amen**

Minister: Let us praise the Lord

People: The Lord's name be praised

Minister:　　　As our saviour Christ has taught us so we pray

All:　Our Father in heaven... .

The Minister may end with the words of grace or if a presbyter is present with benediction.

35.　*Children*

Minister:　　　Our help is in the name of the Lord.

People:　　Who has made heaven and earth.

The Holy Water may be sprinkled on the children to bless.

Reading: Psalm 127 or if appropriate 128.

O Lord our God, you accepted Samuel when he was a little child to serve you and your priest Eli; your Son our Lord Jesus blessed little children saying "let little children come to me do not stop them"; hear our prayer and bless these children (this child _____ (*name*)) that they/*he/she* may grow each day knowing you, loving you and serving you more and more, through Jesus Christ our Lord who lives and reigns with you and the Holy Spirit one God now and forever. **Amen**

Minister:　　　Let us praise the Lord

People:　　The Lord's name be praised

Minister:　　　As our saviour Christ has taught us so we pray

All:　　Our Father in heaven... .

The Minister may end with the words of grace or if a presbyter is present with benediction.

36.　*Choir*

Minister:　　　Our help is in the name of the Lord.

People:　　Who has made heaven and earth.

The Holy Water may be sprinkled on the choir to bless them.

Reading: Psalm 149

Almighty God, you inspired your servant Deborah and Barak to sing and rejoice, you made David to sing with a harp and calm King Saul, your people sang psalms in your Temple in Jerusalem to glorify you; bless O Lord, this choir to praise you and serve your people with their singing so that your congregation may worship you in spirit and in truth; through Jesus Christ our Lord who lives and reigns with you and the Holy Spirit one God now and forever. **Amen**

Minister:	Let us praise the Lord
People:	**The Lord's name be praised**

Minister:	As our saviour Christ has taught us so we pray
All:	**Our Father in heaven... .**

The Minister may end with the words of grace or if a presbyter is present with benediction.

37.   *Christmas Cake(s)*

Minister:	Our help is in the name of the Lord.
People:	**Who has made heaven and earth.**

The Holy Water may be sprinkled on the cakes to bless them.

Reading: Psalm 78.12 -25

O Lord our God, through your mercy your people received manna in the desert and make cakes from it, bless this/these Christmas cake(s) so that those who eat may joyfully celebrate your birth and be nourished in their bodies; through Jesus Christ our Lord who lives and reigns with you and the Holy Spirit one God now and forever. **Amen**

Minister:	Let us praise the Lord
People:	**The Lord's name be praised**

Minister: As our saviour Christ has taught us so we pray

All: **Our Father in heaven... .**

The Minister may end with the words of grace or if a presbyter is present with benediction.

38.   *Christmas tree*

Minister: Our help is in the name of the Lord.

People: **Who has made heaven and earth.**

The Holy Water may be sprinkled on the Christmas.

Reading: Psalm 1

Ever-living and life-giving God, your only begotten Son Jesus died on a tree so that we may receive life. You also promised tree-of-life with twelve kinds of fruits for all seasons in the New Jerusalem and its leaves for healing the nations; bless this Christmas tree, O Lord, to remind us of the great atoning sacrifice of your Son on the tree to give us life and happiness, and bless our efforts to love, protect and grow more trees; through Jesus Christ our Lord who lives and reigns with you and the Holy Spirit one God now and forever. **Amen**

Minister: Let us praise the Lord

People: **The Lord's name be praised**

Minister: As our saviour Christ has taught us so we pray

All: **Our Father in heaven... .**

The Minister may end with the words of grace or if a presbyter is present with benediction.

39.   *Church*

Minister: Our help is in the name of the Lord.

People: **Who has made heaven and earth.**

The Holy Water may be sprinkled in the Church floors and walls and altar and the people to bless.

Reading: Psalm 15

Holy are you, Lord our God, you call people to assemble in your name to praise and worship you; hear our prayer and bless this assembly and this House of prayer where we assemble so that freed from all bondage we may worship you in spirit and in truth; through Jesus Christ our Lord who lives and reigns with you and the Holy Spirit one God now and forever. **Amen**

People:	**The Lord's name be praised**
Minister:	As our saviour Christ has taught us so we pray
All:	**Our Father in heaven... .**

The Minister may end with the words of grace or if a presbyter is present with benediction.

40.   *City (town)*

Minister:	Our help is in the name of the Lord.
People:	**Who has made heaven and earth.**

Reading: Psalm 122

Holy are you, Lord our God, in your mercy you spared Nineveh and taught Jonah how much you loved and cared for its people and cattle; bless this city (_____ *name*) and send forth your Holy Spirit to guard it and to guide it so that its people may follow the way of justice, righteousness and loving-kindness, so that they may dwell in peace and deal compassionately with foreigners among them. Bless this city to prosper in trade, flourish in culture and thrive in Godly knowledge; through Jesus Christ our Lord who lives and reigns with you and the Holy Spirit one God now and forever. **Amen**

Minister:	Let us praise the Lord
People:	**The Lord's name be praised**

Minister:	As our saviour Christ has taught us so we pray
All:	**Our Father in heaven... .**

The Minister may end with the words of grace or if a presbyter is present with benediction.

41. Classroom

Minister:	Our help is in the name of the Lord.
People:	**Who has made heaven and earth.**

The Holy Water may be sprinkled in the class room(s) to bless it.

Reading: Psalm 119. 97-112.

O Lord our God, you teach us deep truths in the nature around us, hear our prayer and bless this class room constructed to teach so that all who learn here may be strengthened in their intellect with knowledge and information; may those who teach and those who learn may come to know you as their source and fountain of knowledge; through Jesus Christ our Lord who lives and reigns with you and the Holy Spirit one God now and forever. Amen

People:	**The Lord's name be praised**
Minister:	As our saviour Christ has taught us so we pray
All:	**Our Father in heaven... .**

The Minister may end with the words of grace or if a presbyter is present with benediction.

42. Clinic

Minister:	Our help is in the name of the Lord.
People:	**Who has made heaven and earth.**

The Holy Water may be sprinkled in the clinic and all those who serve there.

Reading: Psalm 38

Almighty God, your Son our Lord Jesus Christ is the great physician who inspired my physicians like Saint Luke to follow him. The saints and faithful believers wonderful examples for us to serve those struck with various kinds of diseases: to treat them, to take care of them and to heal them in the name of your Son Jesus; bless O Lord we pray, this clinic by sending your Holy Spirit to empower those who work here so that they may excel to serve your people with commitment and compassion; through Jesus Christ our Lord who lives and reigns with you and the Holy Spirit one God now and forever. **Amen**

Minister:	Let us praise the Lord
People:	**The Lord's name be praised**

Minister:	As our saviour Christ has taught us so we pray
All:	**Our Father in heaven... .**

The Minister may end with the words of grace or if a presbyter is present with benediction.

43.   *Clock*

Minister:	Our help is in the name of the Lord.
People:	**Who has made heaven and earth.**

The Holy Water may be sprinkled on the clock (watch) and the people to bless them.

Reading: Psalm 34.1-10

Lord our God, you transcend time and caused the shadow of Sun on the stairs to go back ten steps as a sign for your servant Ahaz, yet for our salvation you accomplished all things within time and have given us the ability to measure it; hear our prayer and bless this clock (watch) to accurately measure our days and nights enabling us, your servants, to go about our work with efficiency; through Jesus Christ our Lord who lives and

reigns with you and the Holy Spirit one God now and forever.
Amen

Minister: Let us praise the Lord

People: **The Lord's name be praised**

Minister: As our saviour Christ has taught us so we pray

All: **Our Father in heaven... .**

The Minister may end with the words of grace or if a presbyter is present with benediction.

44.   *Clothes*

Minister: Our help is in the name of the Lord.

People: **Who has made heaven and earth.**

The Holy Water may be sprinkled on the clothes and the people to bless them.

Reading: Psalm 30

Lord our God, in your mercy you clothe the lilies of the field with splendour surpassing those of the kings, yet your Son our Lord Jesus in the manger was wrapped in swaddling and at the cross his garment was gambled away; hear our prayer and bless these clothes so that those who wear them may find warmth and dignity; through Jesus Christ our Lord who lives and reigns with you and the Holy Spirit one God now and forever. **Amen**

Minister: Let us praise the Lord

People: **The Lord's name be praised.**

The Minister may end with the words of grace or a presbyter by benediction.

45.   *Conference*

Minister: Our help is in the name of the Lord.

People: Who has made heaven and earth.

The Holy Water may be sprinkled in the Conference Centre to bless it.

Reading: Psalm 111

Lord God, in your mercy you gave wisdom to the Holy Apostles and believers to confer and to find solution to their problems; hear our prayer and bless this conference with abundance of wisdom so that they may find their conferring helpful to build up their capacities, plan out their future, evaluate their performance and resolve their conflicts; through Jesus Christ our Lord who lives and reigns with you and the Holy Spirit one God now and forever. **Amen**

Minister: Let us praise the Lord

People: The Lord's name be praised.

The Minister may end with the words of grace or a presbyter by benediction.

46.   *College*

Minister: Our help is in the name of the Lord.

People: Who has made heaven and earth.

Reading: Psalm 119.9-16

O Lord our God, you are the fountain of all knowledge; hear our prayer and bless this place of learning that the Lecturers, Readers And Professors of this College may be duly guided by wisdom and reason to guide those who learn to the knowledge of truth; through Jesus Christ our Lord who lives and reigns with you and the Holy Spirit one God now and forever. **Amen**

Minister: Let us praise the Lord

People: The Lord's name be praised

Minister: As our saviour Christ has taught us so we pray

All: **Our Father in heaven... .**

The Minister may end with the words of grace or if a presbyter is present with benediction.

47.   Computers

Minister: Our help is in the name of the Lord.

People: **Who has made heaven and earth.**

Reading: Psalm 146

O Lord our God, in your mercy you gave intelligence to human beings to make instruments and implements to work manually and intellectually; bless this computer (laptop or palmtop) we pray and those who use it with wisdom and skill so that this facility may support them in their intellectual endeavours; bless us with the insight to know that all wisdom comes from you; through Jesus Christ our Lord who lives and reigns with you and the Holy Spirit one God now and forever. **Amen**

Minister: Let us praise the Lord

People: **The Lord's name be praised**

Minister: As our saviour Christ has taught us so we pray

All: **Our Father in heaven... .**

The Minister may end with the words of grace or if a presbyter is present with benediction.

48.   Cradle

Minister: Our help is in the name of the Lord.

People: **Who has made heaven and earth.**

The Holy Water may be sprinkled on the cradle (also the parents and baby) to bless them.

Reading: Psalm 139

O Lord our God, from the mouths of babes you have caused your name to be praised; bless this cradle to hold the infant that it may keep them safe, and give them rest and sound sleep and bless us dear Lord with inner comfort to realize that you have known us even when no one could us as we form before our birth and that you care for us, through Jesus Christ our Lord who lives and reigns with you and the Holy Spirit one God now and forever. **Amen**

Minister:	Let us praise the Lord
People:	**The Lord's name be praised**

Minister:	As our saviour Christ has taught us so we pray
All:	**Our Father in heaven... .**

The Minister may end with the words of grace or if a presbyter is present with benediction.

49. *Crops (fruits or vegetables)*

Minister:	Our help is in the name of the Lord.
People:	**Who has made heaven and earth.**

The Holy Water may be sprinkled on the crops (fruits and vegetables) and the cultivators to bless them.

Reading: Psalm 67

O Lord our God, you have blessed the earth to bring forth crops, fruits and vegetation in due season; hear our prayer and bless this crop (fruit or vegetables) new ready to be gathered that it may provide nourishment and life to all so that none would starve for lack of food, through Jesus Christ our Lord who lives and reigns with you and the Holy Spirit one God now and forever. **Amen.**

Minister:	Let us praise the Lord
People:	**The Lord's name be praised**

Minister:	As our saviour Christ has taught us so we pray
All:	**Our Father in heaven... .**

The Minister may end with the words of grace or if a presbyter is present with benediction.

50.   *Cross*

Minister:	Our help is in the name of the Lord.
People:	**Who has made heaven and earth.**

The Holy Water may be sprinkled on the cross and the people to bless them.

Reading: Psalm 22.23-31

O Lord our God, the King of the universe, almighty and holy; we saw your love for us when your Son our Lord Jesus came into the world in great humility and died for us on a cross shedding his blood on it to save us; bless and hallow this image of cross that it may remind your servant of your great love for us, through Jesus Christ our Lord who lives and reigns with you and the Holy Spirit one God now and forever. **Amen**

Minister:	Let us praise the Lord
People:	**The Lord's name be praised**

Minister:	As our saviour Christ has taught us so we pray
All:	**Our Father in heaven... .**

The Minister may end with the words of grace or if a presbyter is present with benediction.

51.   Crib (Christmas)

Minister:	Our help is in the name of the Lord.
People:	**Who has made heaven and earth.**

The Holy Water may be sprinkled on the crib and it can be incensed to bless it.

Reading: Psalm 8

O God the Son, highest and holiest, who dist humble yourself to share our birth and our death; Bring us with the shepherds and the sages to kneel before your lowly cradle, that we may come to sing with your angels thy glorious praise in heaven; where with the Father and the Holy Spirit you live and reign one God world without end. Amen.

In the faith of Christ and in your name, O God most Holy, do we bless and hallow this Crib of Christmas to set before the eyes of your children and servants the great love and great humility of Jesus Christ your only Son; to whom with you and the same Spirit be all honour, majesty, glory and worship, now and always. **Amen**.

Minister:	Let us praise the Lord
People:	**The Lord's name be praised**

Minister:	As our saviour Christ has taught us so we pray
All:	**Our Father in heaven... .**

The Minister may end with the words of grace or a presbyter with benediction.

52.   Crockery and Cutlery

Minister:	Our help is in the name of the Lord.
People:	**Who has made heaven and earth.**

The Holy Water may be sprinkled on the crockery and cutlery and the people to bless them.

Reading: Psalm 145.15-21

O Lord our God, through your mercy we have food to eat, bless this crockery and cutlery so that it may be used to serve courses of meals; may our fellowship around the table strengthen bond of kinship and may the ministry of hospitality make strangers to become friends, through Jesus Christ our Lord who lives and reigns with you and the Holy Spirit one God now and forever. **Amen**

Minister:	Let us praise the Lord
People:	**The Lord's name be praised**

Minister:	As our saviour Christ has taught us so we pray
All:	**Our Father in heaven... .**

The Minister may end with the words of grace or if a presbyter is present with benediction.

53. *Crucifer (the one who holds the processional cross)*

Minister:	Our help is in the name of the Lord.
People:	**Who has made heaven and earth.**

The Holy Water may be sprinkled on crucifer and the cross he/she would carry in procession.

Reading: Psalm 22.23-31

O Lord our God, the King of the universe, almighty and holy; we saw your love for us when your Son our Lord Jesus came into the world in great humility and died for us on a cross; hear our prayer and bless this your servant who will carry the cross in processions and ceremonies, and for the announcement of the Gospel that it may remind your people of your great love for us, through Jesus Christ our Lord who lives and reigns with you and the Holy Spirit one God now and forever. **Amen**

Minister:	Let us praise the Lord
People:	**The Lord's name be praised**

Minister:	As our saviour Christ has taught us so we pray
All:	**Our Father in heaven... .**

The Minister may end with the words of grace or if a presbyter is present with benediction.

54.   *Ciborium (a sacred vessel to keep the holy bread of Communion)*

Minister:	Our help is in the name of the Lord.
People:	**Who has made heaven and earth.**

The Holy Water may be sprinkled on the ciborium to bless it.

Reading: Psalm 81

Bless, O heavenly Father this ciborium which we bless in your name; and grant that through its use in the ministration of the Holy Bread at the Eucharist your servant may be brought to a living union with you always being reminded of the suffering love of Jesus your Son our Lord, who lives and reign with you and the Holy Spirit one God now and forever. **Amen**.

Minister:	Let us praise the Lord
People:	**The Lord's name be praised**

Minister:	As our Saviour Christ has taught us so we pray
All:	**Our Father in heaven... .**

The Minister may end with the words of grace or a presbyter with benediction.

55.   *Council*

Minister:	Our help is in the name of the Lord.
People:	**Who has made heaven and earth.**

Reading: Psalm 82

Almighty God, you have generously given us your Holy Spirit as our teacher and guide; bless all the members of our Council (or Synod etc) with wisdom so that they may consult together for the good for your church ; through Jesus Christ our Lord, who lives and reigns with you and the Holy Spirit one God now and forever. **Amen**.

Minister: Let us praise the Lord

People: **The Lord's name be praised**

Minister: As our saviour Christ has taught us so we pray

All: **Our Father in heaven... .**

The Minister may end with the words of grace or if a presbyter is present with benediction.

D

56.   *Defence units*

Minister: Our help is in the name of the Lord.

People: **Who has made heaven and earth.**

Reading: Psalm 3

O Lord our God of hosts, in the days of old you stood with your heavenly armies to defend your people from their enemies; bless this defence unit/regiment we pray with valour and its commandants with wisdom, imbue them with courage and discipline, loyalty and love for the country; let them defend the people with fairness, honour the convention of war, refrain from unjust actions, respect the 'enemy' also as soldiers of the other country, protect civilians on all sides and eagerly work for a future when wars will cease and there will be peace among all people; through Jesus Christ our Lord, who lives and reigns with you and the Holy Spirit one God now and forever. **Amen**.

Minister:	Let us praise the Lord
People:	**The Lord's name be praised**

Minister:	As our saviour Christ has taught us so we pray
All:	**Our Father in heaven... .**

The Minister may end with the words of grace or if a presbyter is present with benediction.

57.   *Dining table*

Minister:	Our help is in the name of the Lord.
People:	**Who has made heaven and earth.**

The Holy Water may be sprinkled on the dining table to bless it.

Reading: Psalm 104.24-35

O Lord our gracious God, in your mercy we have fruits of the earth and you give us our food when it is due; bless we pray this dining table and all those who eat and drink at it so that they may be tied in joyful fellowship and true friendship, and praise you with thankful hearts; through Jesus Christ our Lord, who lives and reigns with you and the Holy Spirit one God now and forever. **Amen.**

Minister:	Let us praise the Lord
People:	**The Lord's name be praised**

Minister:	As our saviour Christ has taught us so we pray
All:	**Our Father in heaven... .**

The Minister may end with the words of grace or a presbyter if present with benediction.

58.   *Doctors*

Minister:	Our help is in the name of the Lord.
People:	**Who has made heaven and earth.**

The Holy Water may be sprinkled on the doctors to bless them.

Reading: Psalm 121

O Lord our God, your Son Jesus our Lord healed the sick and commissioned us to carry forward this work in the world; bless our doctors we pray with strength, wisdom, skill and diligence to attend and relieve the suffering people from their ailments; through Jesus Christ our Lord who lives and reigns with you and the Holy Spirit one God now and always. **Amen.**

Minister:	Let us praise the Lord
People:	**The Lord's name be praised**

Minister:	As our Saviour Christ has taught us so we pray
All:	**Our Father in heaven... .**

The Minister may end with the words of grace or if a presbyter is present with benediction.

59. *Door*

Minister:	Our help is in the name of the Lord.
People:	**Who has made heaven and earth.**

The Holy Water may be sprinkled on the door to bless it.

Reading: Psalm 100

O Lord our God, your Son our Lord Jesus said that he was the door of the sheepfold wherein his sheep found refuge and were protected from destruction; bless this door we pray that it may keep this place, all those who dwell therein and all that is kept in it, secure from ravage and damage; through Jesus Christ our Lord, who lives and reigns with you and the Holy Spirit one God now and forever. **Amen.**

Minister:	Let us praise the Lord
People:	**The Lord's name be praised**

Minister: As our saviour Christ has taught us so we pray

All: Our Father in heaven... .

The Minister may end with the words of grace or if a presbyter is present with benediction.

60.   *Drama*

Minister: Our help is in the name of the Lord.

People: Who has made heaven and earth.

The Holy Water may be sprinkled on the cast to bless them.

Reading: Psalm 78.1-8

O Lord our God, you communicated your message to us human beings through your servants for our good, which your prophets brought in dramatic ways; bless this cast, we pray, for this performance with wisdom, stamina, skill and memory to bring out the message of this drama with clarity; bless the supporting group who are responsible for arrangement behind the stage for makeup, lights, sound and effects, the prompters and the director and all others who are associated with it; through Jesus Christ our Lord, who lives and reigns with you and the Holy Spirit one God now and forever. **Amen.**

Minister: Let us praise the Lord

People: The Lord's name be praised

Minister: As our saviour Christ has taught us so we pray

All: Our Father in heaven... .

The Minister may end with the words of grace or if a presbyter is present with benediction.

E

61.   *Easter Eggs*

Minister: Our help is in the name of the Lord.

People: **Who has made heaven and earth.**

The Holy Water may be sprinkled on the Easter eggs to bless them.

Reading: Psalm 118

O Lord our God, you resurrected Christ from the dead and brought him out of the grave and made life to triumph over death; hear our prayer and bless these Easter eggs which symbolise to us the bursting of grave and triumph of life; through Jesus Christ our Lord, who lives and reigns with you and the Holy Spirit one God now and forever. **Amen**.

Minister: Let us praise the Lord

People: **The Lord's name be praised**

Minister: As our saviour Christ has taught us so we pray

All: **Our Father in heaven... .**

The Minister may end with the words of grace or if a presbyter is present with benediction.

62.   *Electronic goods*

Minister: Our help is in the name of the Lord.

People: **Who has made heaven and earth.**

O Lord our God, in your mercy you have created all things in this world and endowed the earth with potential of power, bless we pray this electronic gadget so that it may serve the purpose for which it has been made and keep them safe who use it; through Jesus Christ our Lord, who lives and reigns with you and the Holy Spirit one God now and forever. **Amen**.

Minister:	Let us praise the Lord
People:	**The Lord's name be praised**

Minister:	As our saviour Christ has taught us so we pray
All:	**Our Father in heaven... .**

The Minister may end with the words of grace or if a presbyter is present with benediction.

63.   *Engineers*

Minister:	Our help is in the name of the Lord.
People:	**Who has made heaven and earth.**

The Holy Water may be sprinkled on the engineers to bless them.

Reading: Psalm 19

O Lord our God, in your kindness you endowed human being with ability to produce and build with scientific precision within the frame of laws which you have set to govern nature and life; hear our prayer and bless these engineers so that they may with wisely employ their skill in their specialized fields to enhance progress in the world in which we live; through Jesus Christ our Lord, who lives and reigns with you and the Holy Spirit one God now and forever. **Amen.**

Minister:	Let us praise the Lord
People:	**The Lord's name be praised**

Minister:	As our saviour Christ has taught us so we pray
All:	**Our Father in heaven... .**

The Minister may end with the words of grace or if a presbyter is present with benediction.

64.   *Equipments*

Minister: Our help is in the name of the Lord.

People: **Who has made heaven and earth.**

The Holy Water may be sprinkled on the equipments to bless them.

Reading: Psalm 150

O Lord our God, you created the world out of nothing with the power of your word, and you have made us to work in fields and factories, in offices and industry with water and soil, wind and light. You gave us intelligence to make instruments of music and equipments for our work and industry; bless we pray these equipments (to be used in agriculture or construction or factory etc._____) for the purpose they have been made so that these may lighten the burden of work, maintain the standard of quality and give a good finish to the product; through Jesus Christ our Lord, who lives and reigns with you and the Holy Spirit one God now and forever. **Amen**.

Minister: Let us praise the Lord

People: **The Lord's name be praised**

Minister: As our saviour Christ has taught us so we pray

All: **Our Father in heaven... .**

The Minister may end with the words of grace or if a presbyter is present with benediction.

65.   *Event*

Minister: Our help is in the name of the Lord.

People: **Who has made heaven and earth.**

The Holy Water may be sprinkled to bless those gathered for the event.

Reading: Psalm 78.1-8

O Lord our God, in your mercy you intervene human history to decisively reorder and reorient us in your way of justice, righteousness and loving kindness and you have implanted creativity in us, giving us the ability to organize events for enhancing our knowledge, enriching our culture and strengthening our social bonds; hear our prayer and bless this (convention/rally/procession/demonstration etc. _____ *name the event*) so that it may succeed to serve the purpose for which it is organized; may your blessing be on those who have organized it and those who participate in it and may their endeavour bear fruit; through Jesus Christ our Lord, who lives and reigns with you and the Holy Spirit one God now and forever. **Amen.**

Minister:	Let us praise the Lord
People:	**The Lord's name be praised**

Minister:	As our saviour Christ has taught us so we pray
All:	**Our Father in heaven... .**

The Minister may end with the words of grace or if a presbyter is present with benediction.

66.   *Exhibition*

Minister:	Our help is in the name of the Lord.
People:	**Who has made heaven and earth.**

The Holy Water may be sprinkled at exhibits or the entrance of the exhibition hall to bless it.

Reading: Psalm 77.5-15

O Lord our God, you have implanted creativity in us, giving us the ability to organize events for enhancing our knowledge, enriching our culture and strengthening our social bonds; hear our prayer and bless this exhibition so that it may succeed to serve the purpose for which it is organized; may your blessing be on those who have organized it and those who come to see it that they may recall and remember, realize and appreciate the ability of those whose work is exhibited here; through Jesus Christ our Lord, who lives and reigns with you and the Holy Spirit one God now and forever. **Amen**

Minister: Let us praise the Lord

People: The Lord's name be praised

Minister: As our saviour Christ has taught us so we pray

All: Our Father in heaven... .

The Minister may end with the words of grace or if a presbyter is present with benediction.

F

67.   *Factory*

Minister: Our help is in the name of the Lord.

People: Who has made heaven and earth.

The Holy Water may be sprinkled the factory or the entrance of the factory and those who work there to bless them.

Reading: Psalm 92

O Lord our God, you have given us the ability of produce things to meet our physical needs; hear our prayer and bless this factory set up for the production of _____ (*name the product*), bless those who manage and those who work here to manufacture with wisdom and skill to run this unit with efficiency; may their toils bring good dividend, may the relationship between the owners and workers be just and the atmosphere be conducive to work; through Jesus Christ our Lord, who lives and reigns with you and the Holy Spirit one God now and forever. **Amen**

Minister:	Let us praise the Lord
People:	**The Lord's name be praised**

Minister:	As our saviour Christ has taught us so we pray
All:	**Our Father in heaven... .**

The Minister may end with the words of grace or if a presbyter is present with benediction.

68.   *Faculty*

Minister:	Our help is in the name of the Lord.
People:	**Who has made heaven and earth.**

The Holy Water may be sprinkled on the members of the faculty to bless them.

Reading: Psalm 19

O Lord our God, the fountain of all knowledge, in your mercy you have made us capable to reason, research and teach; hear our prayer and bless the members of this faculty with ability to teach and to guide their students with diligence and skill so that by their work much would be gained; through Jesus Christ our Lord, who lives and reigns with you and the Holy Spirit one God now and forever. **Amen.**

Minister:	Let us praise the Lord
People:	**The Lord's name be praised**

Minister:	As our saviour Christ has taught us so we pray
All:	**Our Father in heaven... .**

The Minister may end with the words of grace or if a presbyter is present with benediction.

69. *Family*

Minister: Our help is in the name of the Lord.

People: **Who has made heaven and earth.**

The Holy Water may be sprinkled on the family members to bless them.

Reading: Psalm 147.12-20, or 144.9-15

Blessed are you, O Lord our God, in your mercy you provided family for the good purpose in the human race for growth, love, companionship, helpfulness and care; hear our prayer and bless _____ *(head of the family)* and this family that their bonds of love and unity may ever grow stronger, that they may together have the strength to face challenges of life and that their joy may be fulfilled in knowing you, loving you and serving you all the days of their life; through Jesus Christ our Lord, who lives and reigns with you and the Holy Spirit one God now and forever. **Amen.**

Minister: Let us praise the Lord

People: **The Lord's name be praised**

Minister: As our saviour Christ has taught us so we pray

All: **Our Father in heaven... .**

The Minister may end with the words of grace or if a presbyter is present with benediction.

70. *Fan*

Minister: Our help is in the name of the Lord.

People: **Who has made heaven and earth.**

The Holy Water may be sprinkled on the fan to bless it.

O Lord our God, you have set rules for the material world to operate and have made us capable to find, understand and use them for our purpose; bless this fan so that by its operation it may bring relief to the people from hot weather conditions; through Jesus Christ our Lord, who lives and reigns with you and the Holy Spirit one God now and forever. **Amen**

| Minister: | Let us praise the Lord |
| **People:** | **The Lord's name be praised** |

| Minister: | As our saviour Christ has taught us so we pray |
| **All:** | **Our Father in heaven... .** |

The Minister may end with the words of grace or if a presbyter is present with benediction.

71. *Farm*

| Minister: | Our help is in the name of the Lord. |
| **People:** | **Who has made heaven and earth.** |

The Holy Water may be sprinkled on some part of the farm to bless it.

Reading: Psalm 147.1-11

O Lord our God, the creator of the world, you have made us in your image to work and gave land to us for this purpose; hear our prayer and bless this farm so that it may yield good crop and your people would find nourishment and strength and with joyful heart given you praise. (May there be a fair sharing of its fruits between its owner and the cultivators so that none be hungry); through Jesus Christ our Lord, who lives and reigns with you and the Holy Spirit one God now and forever. **Amen**

| Minister: | Let us praise the Lord |
| **People:** | **The Lord's name be praised** |

| Minister: | As our saviour Christ has taught us so we pray |
| **All:** | **Our Father in heaven... .** |

The Minister may end with the words of grace or if a presbyter is present with benediction.

72.   *Fields*

Minister: Our help is in the name of the Lord.

People: **Who has made heaven and earth.**

The Holy Water may be sprinkled on some part of the field to bless it.

Reading: Psalm 126

O Lord our God, in your mercy you gave land to us to cultivate and build; hear our prayer and bless this field that the purpose for which it is used may be good and would bring blessing to the people who would utilize it; through Jesus Christ our Lord, who lives and reigns with you and the Holy Spirit one God now and forever. **Amen**

Minister: Let us praise the Lord

People: **The Lord's name be praised**

Minister: As our saviour Christ has taught us so we pray

All: **Our Father in heaven... .**

The Minister may end with the words of grace or if a presbyter is present with benediction.

73.   *Flag*

Minister: Our help is in the name of the Lord.

People: **Who has made heaven and earth.**

The Holy Water may be sprinkled on the flag to bless it.

Reading: Psalm 138

O Lord our God, you gave signs to the people to reaffirm the promises of your covenant; hear our prayer and bless this flag so that what it signifies may be of help to the people; through

Jesus Christ our Lord, who lives and reigns with you and the Holy Spirit one God now and forever. **Amen**

Minister: Let us praise the Lord

People: The Lord's name be praised

Minister: As our saviour Christ has taught us so we pray

All: Our Father in heaven... .

The Minister may end with the words of grace or if a presbyter is present with benediction.

74.   *Flowers*

Minister: Our help is in the name of the Lord.

People: Who has made heaven and earth.

The Holy Water may be sprinkled on the flowers to bless them.

Reading: Song of Solomon 2.12-16

O Lord our gracious God, in your mercy you created all the flowers with beauty; hear our prayer and bless these flowers so that their use may meaningfully bring joy, delight and express our love; through Jesus Christ our Lord, who lives, and reigns with you and the Holy Spirit one God now and forever. **Amen**

Minister: Let us praise the Lord

People: The Lord's name be praised

Minister: As our saviour Christ has taught us so we pray

All: Our Father in heaven... .

The Minister may end with the words of grace or if a presbyter is present with benediction.

75. *Flowerbed/Flower pot*

Minister: Our help is in the name of the Lord.

People: **Who has made heaven and earth.**

The Holy Water may be sprinkled on the flower beds to bless it.

Reading: Song of Solomon 2.1-7

O Lord our God, you created the earth to bring forth all plants of flower to bring cheer to us; bless this flowerbed (or flower pot) we pray and grant that it may nourish the seeds and plants to bring forth beautiful flowers, bless those who cultivate it with labour so that their work would bring cheer and happiness to many and preserve the law of nature and environment; through Jesus Christ our Lord, who lives and reigns with you and the Holy Spirit one God now and forever. **Amen**

Minister: Let us praise the Lord

People: The Lord's name be praised

Minister: As our saviour Christ has taught us so we pray

All: **Our Father in heaven... .**

The Minister may end with the words of grace or if a presbyter is present with benediction.

76. *Font (for baptizing)*

Minister: Our help is in the name of the Lord.

People: **Who has made heaven and earth.**

The Holy Water may be sprinkled at exhibits or the entrance of the exhibition hall to bless it.

Reading: Psalm 11

Blessed are you, O Lord our God, in your mercy you chose Moses your servant to bring your people safely through the waters red sea, you chose John the Baptist to baptize people who repented of their sins and made baptism the sign for all people to enter the church; bless, O Lord, and sanctify this font which is set apart for administering the sacrament of baptism, the sign to assure us of your grace and our salvation; through Jesus Christ our Lord, who lives and reigns with you and the Holy Spirit one God now and forever. **Amen**

Minister:	Let us praise the Lord
People:	**The Lord's name be praised**

Minister:	As our saviour Christ has taught us so we pray
All:	**Our Father in heaven... .**

The Minister may end with the words of grace or if a presbyter is present with benediction.

77.   *Food*

Minister:	Our help is in the name of the Lord.
People:	**Who has made heaven and earth.**

Reading: Psalm 145.13-21

O Lord our God, the creator and owner of this world in your mercy you provide food from the earth in due season for all creatures who look to you for help; bless we pray this food the produce of the earth and the fruit of human labour; bless those who cultivate fields may they and their families never lack food in their homes; through Jesus Christ our Lord, who lives and reigns with you and the Holy Spirit one God now and forever. **Amen**

Minister:	Let us praise the Lord
People:	**The Lord's name be praised**

Minister:	As our saviour Christ has taught us so we pray
All:	**Our Father in heaven... .**

The Minister may end with the words of grace or if a presbyter is present with benediction.

78. *Fountain (water)*

Minister: Our help is in the name of the Lord.

People: **Who has made heaven and earth.**

The Holy Water may be sprinkled on the fountain to bless it.

Reading: Psalm 93

Blessed are you, O Lord our God, you made Tigris and Euphrates rivers to flow through the garden to Eden to refresh the vegetation and animals; you showed to John your servant the water-of-life flowing through the new Jerusalem and in this way you made water to a sign of new life and hope for us; bless this fountain O Lord we pray that the water flowing in it may bring delight and refreshment to us, may it ever remind us of your promise of new life for us in eternity with your Son Jesus who gives us the water of life; through the same Jesus Christ our Lord, who lives and reigns with you and the Holy Spirit one God now and forever. **Amen**

Minister: Let us praise the Lord

People: **The Lord's name be praised**

Minister: As our saviour Christ has taught us so we pray

All: **Our Father in heaven... .**

The Minister may end with the words of grace or if a presbyter is present with benediction.

79. *Foundation of a building (or the foundation stone)*

Minister: Our help is in the name of the Lord.

People: **Who has made heaven and earth.**

The Holy Water may be sprinkled foundation of the building to bless it.

Reading: Psalm 127.1-2

Blessed are you, O Lord our God, you gave skills, intelligence and strength to King Solomon to undertake the construction of your Temple and Nehemiah your servant to oversee the work of rebuilding the walls of your holy city of Jerusalem; bless, O Lord we pray, the foundation (or the foundation stone) of this building and the intention of our work; forgive us the destruction of nature and despoiling of the habitats of all your creatures who live here for building these foundation; bless all the workers and masons with health and strength and grant that whatever is accomplish may bring you the glory; through Jesus Christ our Lord, who lives and reigns with you and the Holy Spirit one God now and forever. **Amen**

Minister: Let us praise the Lord

People: **The Lord's name be praised**

Minister: As our saviour Christ has taught us so we pray

All: **Our Father in heaven... .**

The Minister may end with the words of grace or if a presbyter is present with benediction.

80.   *Fruits*

Minister: Our help is in the name of the Lord.

People: **Who has made heaven and earth.**

The Holy Water may be sprinkled at exhibits or the entrance of the exhibition hall to bless it.

Reading: Psalm 67

Blessed are you, O Lord our God, in your goodness you planted all kinds of fruit trees in the Garden of Eden and gave it to Adam and Eve to take care of them; bless O Lord we pray this harvest of fruit and grant that it may not rot or deca but it's supply may be efficient and quick so that people may be nourished; through Jesus Christ our Lord, who lives and reigns with you and the Holy Spirit one God now and forever. **Amen**

Minister:	Let us praise the Lord
People:	**The Lord's name be praised**

Minister:	As our saviour Christ has taught us so we pray
All:	**Our Father in heaven... .**

The Minister may end with the words of grace or if a presbyter is present with benediction.

81. *Fruit Garden*

Minister:	Our help is in the name of the Lord.
People:	**Who has made heaven and earth.**

The Holy Water may be sprinkled in the orchard to bless it.

Reading: Psalm 96

Blessed are you, O Lord our God, in your goodness you planted all kinds of fruit trees in the Garden of Eden and gave it to Adam and Eve to take care of them; bless O Lord we pray this orchard of fruits that it may remain healthy to yield good harvest in due season so that the life of the birds and animals and human beings may be sustained and nourished; through Jesus Christ our Lord, who lives and reigns with you and the Holy Spirit one God now and forever. **Amen**

Minister:	Let us praise the Lord
People:	**The Lord's name be praised**

Minister:	As our saviour Christ has taught us so we pray
All:	**Our Father in heaven... .**

The Minister may end with the words of grace or if a presbyter is present with benediction.

82.   Furniture

Minister: Our help is in the name of the Lord.

People: Who has made heaven and earth.

The Holy Water may be sprinkled on the piece of furniture to bless it.

Reading: Psalm 105.1-6

O Lord our God, you have endowed your people with skills and commanded that craftsmen be engaged may bring our their best in building the Tabernacle for the glory of your presence; bless we pray this piece of furniture made with diligence and skill of carpenter and those who craft that it may serve the purpose for which it has been made; through Jesus Christ our Lord, who lives and reigns with you and the Holy Spirit one God now and forever. **Amen.**

Minister: Let us praise the Lord

People: The Lord's name be praised

Minister: As our saviour Christ has taught us so we pray

All: Our Father in heaven... .

The Minister may end with the words of grace or if a presbyter is present with benediction.

G

83.   Games

Minister: Our help is in the name of the Lord.

People: Who has made heaven and earth.

The Holy Water may be sprinkled on the participants to bless them.

Reading: Psalm 104.24-26

O Lord our God, our maker, you have created us with physical body and a spirit to play, bless O Lord we pray this event of games that it may bring happiness to the people, build good relationships, forge within us the values of discipline, honesty, cooperation and all that the spirit of games may inspire towards building a better human community; through Jesus Christ our Lord, who lives and reigns with you and the Holy Spirit one God now and forever. **Amen.**

Minister:	Let us praise the Lord
People:	**The Lord's name be praised**

Minister:	As our saviour Christ has taught us so we pray
All:	**Our Father in heaven... .**

The Minister may end with the words of grace or if a presbyter is present with benediction.

84. *Game Equipments*

Minister:	Our help is in the name of the Lord.
People:	**Who has made heaven and earth.**

The Holy Water may be sprinkled on the game equipments to bless them.

Reading: Psalm 104.24-26

O Lord our God, you have given us minds to organize games, bless we pray these equipments for games so that it may help the players to develop greater measure of accuracy and harness their potential to achieve better; through Jesus Christ our Lord, who lives and reigns with you and the Holy Spirit one God now and forever. **Amen.**

Minister:	Let us praise the Lord
People:	**The Lord's name be praised**

Minister: As our saviour Christ has taught us so we pray

All: **Our Father in heaven... .**

The Minister may end with the words of grace or if a presbyter is present with benediction.

85.   *Garden*

Minister: Our help is in the name of the Lord.

People: **Who has made heaven and earth.**

The Holy Water may be sprinkled somewhere in the garden to bless it.

Reading: Psalm 104.10-17

O Lord our God, you created the first garden for Adam and Eve to live in it, to look after it and to eat the fruits of it; bless this we pray and all those who look after it that it may bring happiness not only to human beings but also to birds and animals helping to enrich the environment with greater diversity of species; through Jesus Christ our Lord, who lives and reigns with you and the Holy Spirit one God now and forever. **Amen.**

Minister: Let us praise the Lord

People: **The Lord's name be praised**

Minister: As our saviour Christ has taught us so we pray

All: **Our Father in heaven... .**

The Minister may end with the words of grace or if a presbyter is present with benediction.

86.   *Garments*

Minister: Our help is in the name of the Lord.

People: **Who has made heaven and earth.**

The Holy Water may be sprinkled on wardrobe to bless the garments.

Reading: Psalm 45.13-17

O Lord our God, you in your kindness clothed the first human beings and desire that all people would be clothed with dignity; bless we pray these garments so that those who wear them would be protected from extremes of climate and weather, and that they would be able to live with due dignity with all other people; through Jesus Christ our Lord, who lives and reigns with you and the Holy Spirit one God now and forever. **Amen.**

Minister:	Let us praise the Lord
People:	**The Lord's name be praised**

Minister:	As our saviour Christ has taught us so we pray
All:	**Our Father in heaven... .**

The Minister may end with the words of grace or if a presbyter is present with benediction

87.   *Generator*

Minister:	Our help is in the name of the Lord.
People:	**Who has made heaven and earth.**

The Holy Water may be sprinkled to bless it.

Reading: Psalm 27

O Lord our God, in your mercy you have given us Sun to give us energy every day and you have given us ability to harness energy from magnetic sources for our use; bless we pray this generator for generating electricity for our uses ; through Jesus Christ our Lord, who lives and reigns with you and the Holy Spirit one God now and forever. **Amen.**

Minister:	Let us praise the Lord
People:	**The Lord's name be praised**

| Minister: | As our saviour Christ has taught us so we pray |
| **All:** | **Our Father in heaven... .** |

The Minister may end with the words of grace or if a presbyter is present with benediction.

88.   *Grave*

| Minister: | Our help is in the name of the Lord. |
| **People:** | **Who has made heaven and earth.** |

The Holy Water may be sprinkled on the grave to bless it.

Reading: Psalm 23

O Lord our God, the source of life, in your Son Jesus, you conquered for us the power of death by raising him from the dead; bless this grave we pray to be the peaceful resting-place of the body of your servant/child till the day of our Lord's coming in glory, who now lives and reigns with you and the Holy Spirit one God now and always. **Amen.**

| Minister: | Let us praise the Lord |
| **People:** | **The Lord's name be praised** |

| Minister: | As our saviour Christ has taught us so we pray |
| **All:** | **Our Father in heaven... .** |

The Minister may end with the words of grace or if a presbyter is present with benediction.

89.   *Grounds*

| Minister: | Our help is in the name of the Lord. |
| **People:** | **Who has made heaven and earth.** |

The Holy Water may be sprinkled on the ground to bless it.

Reading: Psalm 24

O Lord our God, in your mercy you gave this earth to Adam to cultivate and to the human beings for their use, bless we pray these grounds set apart for the purpose of (sports or cultivation or construction of a building or specify any other use) so that its use may be for the betterment of your people; through Jesus Christ our Lord, who lives and reigns with you and the Holy Spirit one God now and forever. **Amen.**

| Minister: | Let us praise the Lord |
| **People:** | **The Lord's name be praised** |

| Minister: | As our saviour Christ has taught us so we pray |
| **All:** | **Our Father in heaven... .** |

The Minister may end with the words of grace or if a presbyter is present with benediction.

90. *Guest house*

| Minister: | Our help is in the name of the Lord. |
| **People:** | **Who has made heaven and earth.** |

The Holy Water may be sprinkled in the guest house to bless it.

Reading: Psalm 4

O Lord our God, in your mercy you visited Abraham as a guest and he fed you; bless this Guest house so that those who will live here may find warmth of hospitality and true welcome; and may the hosts meet you in every guest they serve; through Jesus Christ our Lord, who lives and reigns with you and the Holy Spirit one God now and forever. **Amen.**

| Minister: | Let us praise the Lord |
| **People:** | **The Lord's name be praised** |

| Minister: | As our saviour Christ has taught us so we pray |
| **All:** | **Our Father in heaven... .** |

The Minister may end with the words of grace or if a presbyter is present with benediction.

91. Guitar

Minister: Our help is in the name of the Lord.

People: **Who has made heaven and earth.**

The Holy Water may be sprinkled on the guitar to bless it.

Reading: Psalm 150

O Lord our God, you gave skills to people to make harps, trumpets, cymbals and many musical instruments to glorify you; bless this guitar we pray and may those who play it may become more and more accomplished and use their skill to enable your people to lift their hearts in praise and worship to the glory of your name; through Jesus Christ our Lord, who lives and reigns with you and the Holy Spirit one God now and forever. **Amen.**

Minister: Let us praise the Lord

People: **The Lord's name be praised**

Minister: As our saviour Christ has taught us so we pray

All: **Our Father in heaven... .**

The Minister may end with the words of grace or if a presbyter is present with benediction.

92. Gymnasium

Minister: Our help is in the name of the Lord.

People: **Who has made heaven and earth.**

The Holy Water may be sprinkled equipments of the Gymnasium to bless it.

Reading: Psalm 18.1-6

O Lord God, our strength and our dignity, you have made our physical bodies to accomplish your purpose in our life and in our world where we live; bless we pray this gymnasium that people may be enabled to maintain proper fitness of their body and enjoy good health and may be able to accomplish good things; through Jesus Christ our Lord, who lives and reigns with you and the Holy Spirit one God now and forever. **Amen.**

Minister:	Let us praise the Lord
People:	**The Lord's name be praised**

Minister:	As our saviour Christ has taught us so we pray
All:	**Our Father in heaven... .**

The Minister may end with the words of grace or if a presbyter is present with benediction.

H

93. *Hall*

Minister:	Our help is in the name of the Lord.
People:	**Who has made heaven and earth.**

The Holy Water may be sprinkled in some portion of the hall to bless it.

Reading: Psalm 149

O Lord our God, you commanded your people to assemble so that they may be able to build themselves up into a community; bless this hall O Lord and bless the assemblies that will be held here. May the various events that would take place here help people to strengthen their common bonds, develop healthy identify and forge community consciousness; through Jesus Christ our Lord, who lives and reigns with you and the Holy Spirit one God now and forever. **Amen.**

Minister:	Let us praise the Lord
People:	**The Lord's name be praised**

Minister:	As our saviour Christ has taught us so we pray
All:	**Our Father in heaven... .**

The Minister may end with the words of grace or if a presbyter is present with benediction.

94.   *Harvest*

Minister:	Our help is in the name of the Lord.
People:	**Who has made heaven and earth.**

The Holy Water may be sprinkled on some portion of harvest to bless it.

Reading: Psalm 65.9-13

Gracious are you, O Lord our God, through your mercy we have this harvest, the fruit of the earth and of human labour; bless the bounty of this harvest, O Lord, and preserve it from all destruction and decay so that it may be distributed in a manner that all may eat and none be deprived of food, and bless your holy name; through Jesus Christ our Lord, who lives and reigns with you and the Holy Spirit one God now and forever. **Amen.**

Minister:	Let us praise the Lord
People:	**The Lord's name be praised**

Minister:	As our saviour Christ has taught us so we pray
All:	**Our Father in heaven... .**

The Minister may end with the words of grace or if a presbyter is present with benediction.

95.   *Headquarters*

Minister: Our help is in the name of the Lord.

People: Who has made heaven and earth.

The Holy Water may be sprinkled at the entrance of the building to bless it.

Reading: Psalm 66

O Lord our God, you desire that all our work should be done in systematic order; bless O Lord we pray this Headquarters of _____ (name of organization), so that the facilities may here be used to efficiently coordinate all the work undertaken; keep all those who work here secure in body, alert in mind and in good health always being sensitive to the needs of those who work in this organization and those who benefit from their work; through Jesus Christ our Lord, who lives and reigns with you and the Holy Spirit one God now and forever. **Amen.**

Minister: Let us praise the Lord

People: The Lord's name be praised

Minister: As our saviour Christ has taught us so we pray

All: Our Father in heaven... .

The Minister may end with the words of grace or if a presbyter is present with benediction.

96.   *Home*

Minister: Our help is in the name of the Lord.

People: Who has made heaven and earth.

The Holy Water may be sprinkled in the rooms to bless it.

Reading: Psalm 15

Ever loving God, you desire that people should live in their homes and none be homeless; bless this home, O Lord, sanctify and hallow it by your presence that in it there may be charity, peace, humility, kindness, gentleness, health, obedience and thanksgiving to the Father, the Son and the Holy Spirit, and let your blessing come down on those who dwell in it and those who visit, now and forever. **Amen.**

Minister: Let us praise the Lord

People: The Lord's name be praised

Minister: As our saviour Christ has taught us so we pray

All: Our Father in heaven… .

The Minister may end with the words of grace or if a presbyter is present with benediction.

97.   *Home (for the Aged, blind, differently-abled, widows, etc.)*

Minister: Our help is in the name of the Lord.

People: Who has made heaven and earth.

The Holy Water may be sprinkled in the Home to bless it.

Reading: Psalm 37.23-31

Ever caring God, you desire that people should live with dignity and none be homeless; bless this home for the elderly (_____ name the home), O Lord, sanctify and hallow it by your presence that in it there may be charity, peace, humility, care, kindness, gentleness, health, and thanksgiving to the Father, the Son and the Holy Spirit, and let your blessing come down on those who dwell in it and those who visit, now and forever. **Amen.**

Minister: Let us praise the Lord

People: The Lord's name be praised

Minister:	As our saviour Christ has taught us so we pray
All:	**Our Father in heaven... .**

The Minister may end with the words of grace or if a presbyter is present with benediction.

98.   *Hospice*

Minister:	Our help is in the name of the Lord.
People:	**Who has made heaven and earth.**

The Holy Water may be sprinkled in the Hospice to bless it.

Reading: Psalm 39

Holy are you, O Lord our God, you never leave us from the day we are born till after we die; bless, O Lord we pray, this hospice established for the care of dying and all those who take care of those who are here that in them they meet our living Lord and those who are cared may know the loving and healing touch of resurrected Christ; through the same Jesus Christ our Lord, who lives and reigns with you and the Holy Spirit one God now and forever. **Amen.**

Minister:	Let us praise the Lord
People:	**The Lord's name be praised**

Minister:	As our saviour Christ has taught us so we pray
All:	**Our Father in heaven... .**

The Minister may end with the words of grace or if a presbyter is present with benediction.

99.   *Hospital*

Minister:	Our help is in the name of the Lord.
People:	**Who has made heaven and earth.**

The Holy Water may be sprinkled at the entrance of the Hospital building to bless it.

Reading: Psalm 41

All healing of our treatment comes from you, O Lord our God, for in you we live and move and have our being; bless O Lord we pray this hospital, and all its facilities and equipments; bless those who treat and all those who are treated here; we pray for your blessings on the procedures of treatment that are undertaken here; grant diligence and alertness of mind to all those to take care of the patients; through Jesus Christ our Lord, who lives and reigns with you and the Holy Spirit one God now and forever. **Amen.**

Minister:	Let us praise the Lord
People:	**The Lord's name be praised**

Minister:	As our saviour Christ has taught us so we pray
All:	**Our Father in heaven... .**

The Minister may end with the words of grace or if a presbyter is present with benediction.

100.   *Hostel*

Minister:	Our help is in the name of the Lord.
People:	**Who has made heaven and earth.**

The Holy Water may be sprinkled to bless the hostel and those who live in it.

Reading: Psalm 15

O Lord our God, you love knowledge and discipline; bless _____ (name of the hostel) for your glory and hallow it by your presence so that the children who live here may be formed in human virtues through the good discipline and faith in Christ, through Jesus Christ our Lord, who lives and reigns with you and the Holy Spirit one God now and forever. **Amen.**

Minister:	Let us praise the Lord
People:	**The Lord's name be prai**sed

Minister:	As our saviour Christ has taught us so we pray
All:	**Our Father in heaven... .**

The Minister may end with the words of grace or if a presbyter is present with benediction.

101. Hotel

Minister:	Our help is in the name of the Lord.
People:	**Who has made heaven and earth.**

The Holy Water may be sprinkled on the piece of furniture to bless it.

Reading: Psalm 23

O Lord our God, your prophet Elisha accepted the hospitality of the family at Shunem, but Mary had none to welcome her in Bethlehem for there was no place in the inn except the cattle shed to shelter her and a manger to keep her holy infant; pour out your blessing on this hotel that it may provide rest to the weary and be a place of welcome and comfort to the travellers; through Jesus Christ our Lord, who lives and reigns with you and the Holy Spirit one God now and forever. **Amen.**

Minister:	Let us praise the Lord
People:	**The Lord's name be praised**

Minister:	As our saviour Christ has taught us so we pray
All:	**Our Father in heaven... .**

The Minister may end with the words of grace or if a presbyter is present with benediction.

102.   *Hymn Book(s)*

Minister: Our help is in the name of the Lord.

People: Who has made heaven and earth.

The Holy Water may be sprinkled on the hymn books to bless them.

Reading: Psalm 95

O Lord our God, you have given your creatures gift to sing and endowed human beings and angels with ability to sing your praises, bless and sanctify these Hymn Books(s) containing the hymns which your inspired servants wrote and that through these hymns we may join the celestial company of saints and angels ever praising you singing Alleluia; and that the singling of these hymns may inspire us to love you ever more; through Jesus Christ our Lord, who lives and reigns with you and the Holy Spirit one God now and forever. **Amen.**

Minister: Let us praise the Lord

People: The Lord's name be praised

Minister: As our saviour Christ has taught us so we pray

All: Our Father in heaven... .

The Minister may end with the words of grace or if a presbyter is present with benediction.

I

103.   *Implements*

Minister: Our help is in the name of the Lord.

People: Who has made heaven and earth.

The Holy Water may be sprinkled on the implements to bless it.

Reading: Psalm 118.19-29

O Lord our God, who have given this earth to the human beings to work on it and have given us the ability to make tools for work; your Son Jesus also worked with tools as a carpenter in his village; bless O Lord these implements for the work of _____ (carpentry, masonry, farming etc.) that those who use them may find them helpful; through Jesus Christ our Lord, who lives and reigns with you and the Holy Spirit one God now and forever. **Amen.**

Minister:	Let us praise the Lord
People:	**The Lord's name be praised**

Minister:	As our saviour Christ has taught us so we pray
All:	**Our Father in heaven... .**

The Minister may end with the words of grace or if a presbyter is present with benediction.

104. *Industry*

Minister:	Our help is in the name of the Lord.
People:	**Who has made heaven and earth.**

The Holy Water may be sprinkled at the door and in the office and other sections of the industry to bless it.

Reading: Psalm 145

O Lord our God, you made human beings giving them strength and wisdom to meet their requirements from the elements of this earth; bless we pray this industry that with quality and adequate production it may meet the needs of the people; bless those who work and those who manage with stamina and wisdom that in administering this industry they may find fulfilment and meaningfulness in their engagement; through Jesus Christ our Lord, who lives and reigns with you and the Holy Spirit one God now and forever. **Amen.**

Minister: Let us praise the Lord

People: **The Lord's name be praised**

Minister: As our saviour Christ has taught us so we pray

All: **Our Father in heaven... .**

The Minister may end with the words of grace or if a presbyter is present with benediction.

J

105. *Jail*

Minister: Our help is in the name of the Lord.

People: **Who has made heaven and earth.**

Reading: Psalm 130

O Lord our God, it is not your desire that human beings suffer and therefore since the ancient times you set up wise judges to curtail those whose actions bring unjustified misery to others; bless we pray this jail where many are undergoing penalty for their undue deeds   so that the sentence they serve here may bring correction in their behaviour; bless with wisdom those who administer this jail that they should be firm and sensitive to those who are penalized justly for their deeds and also those who are prisoners of conscience; through Jesus Christ our Lord, who lives and reigns with you and the Holy Spirit one God now and forever. **Amen.**

Minister: Let us praise the Lord

People: **The Lord's name be praised**

Minister:	As our saviour Christ has taught us so we pray
All:	**Our Father in heaven... .**

The Minister may end with the words of grace or if a presbyter is present with benediction.

106. *Jewellery*

Minister:	Our help is in the name of the Lord.
People:	**Who has made heaven and earth.**

The Holy Water may be sprinkled on the Jewellery to bless it.

Reading: Psalm 49

O Lord our God, out of love you created this universe endowing us human beings with ability to cherish beautiful things which our eyes see; bless this jewellery, the objects of beauty and the craftsmen who through their labour and skill gave them greater splendour that they may reflect the perfect beauty of their creator where ever they are adorned; through Jesus Christ our Lord, who lives and reigns with you and the Holy Spirit one God now and forever. **Amen.**

Minister:	Let us praise the Lord
People:	**The Lord's name be praised**

Minister:	As our saviour Christ has taught us so we pray
All:	**Our Father in heaven... .**

The Minister may end with the words of grace or if a presbyter is present with benediction.

K

107. *Kitchen*

Minister: Our help is in the name of the Lord.

People: Who has made heaven and earth.

The Holy Water may be sprinkled in the kitchen to bless it.

Reading: Psalm 117

O Lord our God, your Son Jesus said: Which is greater, one who sits at table, or one who serves? But I am among you as one who serves. Lord, grant to all who work in this room that, in serving others, they may serve you, and share in you perfect service, and that in the noise and clatter of the kitchen, they possess you in peace; through Jesus Christ our Lord, who lives and reigns with you and the Holy Spirit one God now and forever. **Amen.**

Minister: Let us praise the Lord

People: The Lord's name be praised

Minister: As our saviour Christ has taught us so we pray

All: Our Father in heaven... .

The Minister may end with the words of grace or if a presbyter is present with benediction.

L

108. *Laboratory*

Minister: Our help is in the name of the Lord.

People: Who has made heaven and earth.

The Holy Water may be sprinkled in the laboratory to bless it.

Reading: Psalm 111

O Lord our God, you gave us this earth and its environment as a gift, and you gave us intelligence and authority to use its provisions as caretakers. Bless this laboratory O Lord we pray that the experiments and research undertaken here may be enhance life in this beautiful earth; through Jesus Christ our Lord, who lives and reigns with you and the Holy Spirit one God now and forever. **Amen.**

Minister:	Let us praise the Lord
People:	**The Lord's name be praised**

Minister:	As our saviour Christ has taught us so we pray
All:	**Our Father in heaven... .**

The Minister may end with the words of grace or if a presbyter is present with benediction.

109. *Labourers*

Minister:	Our help is in the name of the Lord.
People:	**Who has made heaven and earth.**

The Holy Water may be sprinkled on the workers to bless it.

Reading: Psalm 84

O Lord our God, you gave strength to Adam to till the land and enjoy the fruit of harvests. Bless O Lord these sisters and brothers that as they labour to earn a living, you would give them strength, stamina and wisdom; keep them safe in body and health in all that they are undertaking in work and labour; through Jesus Christ our Lord, who lives and reigns with you and the Holy Spirit one God now and forever. **Amen.**

Minister:	Let us praise the Lord
People:	**The Lord's name be praised**

Minister: As our saviour Christ has taught us so we pray

All: **Our Father in heaven... .**

The Minister may end with the words of grace or if a presbyter is present with benediction.

110.   *Lamp*

Minister: Our help is in the name of the Lord.

People: **Who has made heaven and earth.**

The Minister will light the lamp saying:

Minister: In the name of the Father and of the Son and of the Holy Spirit. **Amen**

Reading: Psalm 27

Blessed are you, O Lord our God, you commanded 'let there be light' and the light was created. Bless this lamp O Lord we pray, that the light of its flame may remove the darkness and help people to safely find their way; through Jesus Christ our Lord, who lives and reigns with you and the Holy Spirit one God now and forever. **Amen.**

Minister: Let us praise the Lord

People: **The Lord's name be praised**

Minister: As our saviour Christ has taught us so we pray

All: **Our Father in heaven... .**

The Minister may end with the words of grace or if a presbyter is present with benediction.

111.   *Land*

Minister: Our help is in the name of the Lord.

People: **Who has made heaven and earth.**

The Holy Water may be sprinkled on land to bless it.

Reading: Psalm 24

O Lord our God, you removed the waters of oceans and made the land, you set the boundaries of waters that it may not submerge land and its creatures. Bless O Lord we pray this land so that all that will be undertaken on this land may be for the benefit of all. Forgive us if in our endeavours we unintentionally harm other living creatures; through Jesus Christ our Lord, who lives and reigns with you and the Holy Spirit one God now and forever. **Amen.**

Minister:	Let us praise the Lord
People:	**The Lord's name be praised**

Minister:	As our saviour Christ has taught us so we pray
All:	**Our Father in heaven... .**

The Minister may end with the words of grace or if a presbyter is present with benediction.

112. *Laundry room*

Minister:	Our help is in the name of the Lord.
People:	**Who has made heaven and earth.**

The Holy Water may be sprinkled in the laundry room to bless it.

Reading: Psalm 26

O Lord our God, you desire that all things should be clean and hygienic. Bless we pray this laundry room set up to wash clothes and linen that through its services people may secure hygiene in the things they use daily in their life; through Jesus Christ our Lord, who lives and reigns with you and the Holy Spirit one God now and forever. **Amen.**

Minister:	Let us praise the Lord
People:	**The Lord's name be praised**

Minister: As our saviour Christ has taught us so we pray

All: Our Father in heaven... .

The Minister may end with the words of grace or if a presbyter is present with benediction.

113.   *Library*

Minister: Our help is in the name of the Lord.

People: Who has made heaven and earth.

The Holy Water may be sprinkled in the library to bless it.

Reading: Psalm 119.33-40

Holy are you, O Lord our God, the source of all knowledge, wisdom and learning. You inspired your prophets, priests and sages to write in the ancient times and you gave your Holy Spirit to Apostles and Evangelists to write the gospels and epistles. You have continued to inspire your saints with Spirit and wisdom to become scholars and doctors in order to think, reflect and write. Bless this library O Lord we pray that it may enlighten the minds of your great servants and saintly scholars who reflect and write as their service to your holy people. May the collection of books in this library be a heritage for our learning and scholarship; may the resources of this library enable your servants to know you and be known by you, to love you and be loved by you and to faithfully serve you all their lives; through Jesus Christ our Lord, who lives and reigns with you and the Holy Spirit one God now and forever. **Amen.**

Minister: Let us praise the Lord

People: The Lord's name be praised

Minister: As our saviour Christ has taught us so we pray

All: Our Father in heaven... .

The Minister may end with the words of grace or if a presbyter is present with benediction.

114.   *Lift*

Minister:	Our help is in the name of the Lord.
People:	**Who has made heaven and earth.**

The Holy Water may be sprinkled in the lift to bless it.

Reading: Psalm 123.1-2

O Lord our God, your servant Jacob saw your angels ascending and descending from heaven to earth at Bethel. Bless this lift we pray that it may efficiently accomplish the purpose for which it has been installed. Keep all those people safe who ascend and descend various levels of this building in this lift; through Jesus Christ our Lord, who lives, and reigns with you and the Holy Spirit one God now and forever. **Amen.**

Minister:	Let us praise the Lord
People:	**The Lord's name be praised**

Minister:	As our saviour Christ has taught us so we pray
All:	**Our Father in heaven... .**

The Minister may end with the words of grace or if a presbyter is present with benediction.

115.   *Light*

Minister:	Our help is in the name of the Lord.
People:	**Who has made heaven and earth.**

The Minister switches on the lights of the building and says:

Minister:	May the light of Christ the Sun of righteousness shine on you.
All:	**And scatter the darkness before our paths. Alleluia**

Reading: Psalm 27

Blessed are you, O Lord our God, who created light and said that it was good, who's servant David wrote that 'Your word is a lamp to my feet and a light for my path" and your Son Jesus Christ said 'I am the light of the world those who follow me will not walk in darkness but will have the light of life". Bless we pray O Lord the lights of this building that it may be so illuminate the passages and gangways that the people may walk in safety through this building. Bless those who work in here that these lights may help them to accomplish their tasks with efficiently; through Jesus Christ our Lord, who lives and reigns with you and the Holy Spirit one God now and forever. **Amen.**

Minister:	Let us praise the Lord
People:	**The Lord's name be praised**

Minister:	As our saviour Christ has taught us so we pray
All:	**Our Father in heaven... .**

The Minister may end with the words of grace or if a presbyter is present with benediction.

116.   Linen

Minister:	Our help is in the name of the Lord.
People:	**Who has made heaven and earth.**

The Holy Water may be sprinkled on the linen to bless it.

Reading: Psalm 117

Bless, O Lord our God, this linen now ready to be used [for altar, or bed, or table or_____ (*name*)]. May it give dignity to what it covers; through Jesus Christ our Lord, who lives, and reigns with you and the Holy Spirit one God now and forever. **Amen.**

Minister: Let us praise the Lord

People: **The Lord's name be praised**

Minister: As our saviour Christ has taught us so we pray

All: **Our Father in heaven... .**

The Minister may end with the words of grace or if a presbyter is present with benediction.

M

117. *Match (games)*

Minister: Our help is in the name of the Lord.

People: **Who has made heaven and earth.**

The Holy Water may be sprinkled on the players to bless them.

Reading: Psalm 119.1-8

O Lord our God, our maker, you have created us with physical body and a spirit to play, bless O Lord we pray this match [of cricket or football or volley-ball or basketball or _____ (name the game)] that it may bring happiness to the people, build good relationships, forge within us the values of discipline, honesty, cooperation and all that the spirit of games may inspire towards building a better human community; through Jesus Christ our Lord, who lives and reigns with you and the Holy Spirit one God now and forever. **Amen.**

Minister: Let us praise the Lord

People: **The Lord's name be praised**

Minister: As our saviour Christ has taught us so we pray

All: **Our Father in heaven... .**

The Minister may end with the words of grace or if a presbyter is present with benediction.

118.   Medal

Minister:	Our help is in the name of the Lord.
People:	**Who has made heaven and earth.**

The Holy Water may be sprinkled on the medal(s) to bless it.

Reading: Psalm 103.1-5

O Lord our God, it gives us joy to be appreciated and recognized for the talents that you have given us. Bless this/*these* medal(s) we pray that it/*these* may help us to appropriately express our appreciation for the those who compete and win; through Jesus Christ our Lord, who lives and reigns with you and the Holy Spirit one God now and forever. **Amen.**

Minister:	Let us praise the Lord
People:	**The Lord's name be praised**

Minister:	As our saviour Christ has taught us so we pray
All:	**Our Father in heaven... .**

The Minister may end with the words of grace or if a presbyter is present with benediction.

119.   Medical equipments

Minister:	Our help is in the name of the Lord.
People:	**Who has made heaven and earth.**

Reading: Psalm 6

Gracious God, your Son our Lord Jesus restored to health those who were troubled by diseases. He healed the fever of Peter's mother in law and she got up and served him, he told the man born blind to wash in the pool of Siloam to restore his eye sight. Bless we pray this medical instrument new commissioned for use. Bless all those who use it with efficiency and alertness. So that through their ministrations people may received health and wholeness; through Jesus Christ our Lord, who lives and reigns with you and the Holy Spirit one God now and forever. **Amen.**

Minister: Let us praise the Lord

People: **The Lord's name be praised**

Minister: As our saviour Christ has taught us so we pray

All: **Our Father in heaven... .**

The Minister may end with the words of grace or if a presbyter is present with benediction.

120. *Medical store*

Minister: Our help is in the name of the Lord.

People: **Who has made heaven and earth.**

The Holy Water may be sprinkled in the store to bless it.

Reading: Psalm 6

O Lord our God, you have provided cure for illness in the nature around us and you have given us intelligence to make medicines out of them. Bless you pray this medical store and all the medicines stored here. Bless those who work here with efficiency so that they may carefully store and distribute the medicines to those who are sick for the restoration of their health and wholeness; through Jesus Christ our Lord, who lives and reigns with you and the Holy Spirit one God now and forever. **Amen.**

Minister: Let us praise the Lord

People: **The Lord's name be praised**

Minister: As our saviour Christ has taught us so we pray

All: Our Father in heaven... .

The Minister may end with the words of grace or if a presbyter is present with benediction.

121.   *Money*

Minister: Our help is in the name of the Lord.

People: Who has made heaven and earth.

The Holy Water may be sprinkled on the piece of furniture to bless it.

Reading: Psalm 15

O Lord our God, your early disciples sold all that they had and laid it at the feet of the apostles to distribute to those in need. Bless this money now collected through the good efforts of your servants. Bless it we pray and bless those who are responsible for its use, investment and disbursement so that through its right use many would find help; through Jesus Christ our Lord, who lives and reigns with you and the Holy Spirit one God now and forever. **Amen.**

Minister: Let us praise the Lord

People: The Lord's name be praised

Minister: As our saviour Christ has taught us so we pray

All: Our Father in heaven... .

The Minister may end with the words of grace or if a presbyter is present with benediction.

122.   *Museum*

Minister: Our help is in the name of the Lord.

People: Who has made heaven and earth.

The Holy Water may be sprinkled on the main doors of the museum to bless it.

Reading: Psalm 78.1-4

O Lord our God, your people built tombs for Abraham and Sarah and other great saints to remember them. You have endowed the human being with memories to learn, recall and cherish. Bless this museum O Lord and grant through what is preserved in here we may learn of the things of the past and move on ahead to progress; through Jesus Christ our Lord, who lives and reigns with you and the Holy Spirit one God now and forever. **Amen.**

Minister:	Let us praise the Lord
People:	**The Lord's name be praised**

Minister:	As our saviour Christ has taught us so we pray
All:	**Our Father in heaven... .**

The Minister may end with the words of grace or if a presbyter is present with benediction.

123. *Musical Instruments*

Minister:	Our help is in the name of the Lord.
People:	**Who has made heaven and earth.**

It may be advised that the Holy water not be used if the instrument is an electronic device.

Reading: Psalm 150

O Lord our God, your servant David played the harp and helped King Saul to gain his peace. Bless we pray this instrument that it may help your people to worship you in spirit and in truth to your praise and glory; through Jesus Christ our Lord, who lives and reigns with you and the Holy Spirit one God now and forever. **Amen.**

Minister: Let us praise the Lord

People: The Lord's name be praised

Minister: As our saviour Christ has taught us so we pray

All: Our Father in heaven... .

The Minister may end with the words of grace or if a presbyter is present with benediction.

N

124. *Nurses*

Minister: Our help is in the name of the Lord.

People: Who has made heaven and earth.

Holy water may be sprinkled on the nurses.

Reading: Psalm 18.31-36

O Lord our God, your Son Jesus Christ healed stretched out his hands to heal the sick, the blind and those affected by leprosy. Thorough him you showed us your care for us and your love to restore us to wholeness. Bless O Lord we pray these nurses (of _____(*name of hospital*) with love and commitment, skill and intelligence, wisdom and strength that their service of care may surpass the limit of medical treatment; through Jesus Christ our Lord, who lives and reigns with you and the Holy Spirit one God now and forever. **Amen.**

Minister: Let us praise the Lord

People: The Lord's name be praised

Minister: As our saviour Christ has taught us so we pray

All: Our Father in heaven... .

The Minister may end with the words of grace or if a presbyter is present with benediction.

125. *Nursing (School/College)*

Minister: Our help is in the name of the Lord.

People: **Who has made heaven and earth.**

It may be advised that the Holy water may be sprinkled in the building.

Reading: Psalm 19

O Lord our God, your servants had powers to heal the disease of people. Elijah advised Namaan to bathe in river Jordan and he was healed of this skin disease, Jesus our Lord healed those who had faith, Peter healed the lame man at the Temple's Gate. Your Son gave us authority to heal every disease and bring happiness to people. Bless O Lord this school/College of Nursing. Bless all those who teach and who study here. Bless those who administer this institution that the Nursing students may learn the skill thoroughly and with commitment serve the suffering people and so bring glory to your name; through Jesus Christ our Lord, who lives, and reigns with you and the Holy Spirit one God now and forever. **Amen.**

Minister: Let us praise the Lord

People: **The Lord's name be praised**

Minister: As our saviour Christ has taught us so we pray

All: **Our Father in heaven... .**

The Minister may end with the words of grace or if a presbyter is present with benediction.

O

126. *Offering/Collection Bags*

Minister: Our help is in the name of the Lord.

People: **Who has made heaven and earth.**

The Holy water may be sprinkled on the bags to bless them.

Reading: Psalm 117

O Lord our God, you desire that the gospel of the Kingdom should be preached in all nations. Bless these collection bags O Lord. Bless those who will contribute to the work of your kingdom so that those who faithfully preach of the coming of your kingdom may be sustained and the need of their ministry may be met; through Jesus Christ our Lord, who lives and reigns with you and the Holy Spirit one God now and forever. **Amen.**

Minister: Let us praise the Lord

People: **The Lord's name be praised**

Minister: As our saviour Christ has taught us so we pray

All: **Our Father in heaven... .**

The Minister may end with the words of grace or if a presbyter is present with benediction.

127. *Office*

Minister: Our help is in the name of the Lord.

People: **Who has made heaven and earth.**

The Holy water may be sprinkled in the office to bless it.

Reading: Psalm 100

O Lord our God, after you had finished creating the good world and all that is in it, you gave human beings the authority to take care of it as your representatives. You have given us intelligence to coordinate and to administer and so to take care of this earth, our institutions and our organizations. Bless O Lord we pray this office now set up for administering this institution and all this work; bless those who work in this office with wisdom and energy so that with dedication and commitment they may carry on through his office the good work that this organization/institution stands for; through Jesus Christ our Lord, who lives and reigns with you and the Holy Spirit one God now and forever. **Amen.**

Minister:	Let us praise the Lord
People:	**The Lord's name be praised**

Minister:	As our saviour Christ has taught us so we pray
All:	**Our Father in heaven... .**

The Minister may end with the words of grace or if a presbyter is present with benediction.

128. *Oil for healing*

Minister:	Our help is in the name of the Lord.
People:	**Who has made heaven and earth.**

The oil to be blessed should be placed in a proper vial on the Altar or a table.

Reading: Psalm 42

O Lord our God, your servants anointed sacred places with oil to mark your presence. Jacob anointed the stone at Bethel on which he laid his head to sleep and dreamed the of angels ascending and descending, your holy priest Aaron was anointed to be set apart as your servant in the Tabernacle and your Son Jesus was anointed by a humble woman before his sacrifice on the cross. Bless O Lord, this oil which we now set apart a sign of your presence. Bless your servant who anoints and those who will receive anointing in this oil. Bless them to experience your healing and wholeness in their life and fill them with your heavenly peace; through Jesus Christ our Lord, who lives and reigns with you and the Holy Spirit one God now and forever. **Amen.**

Minister: Let us praise the Lord

People: The Lord's name be praised

Minister: As our saviour Christ has taught us so we pray

All: Our Father in heaven... .

The Minister may end with the words of grace or if a presbyter is present with benediction.

129.   *Oil for Blessing (chrism)*

Minister: Our help is in the name of the Lord.

People: Who has made heaven and earth.

The oil to be blessed should be placed in a proper vial on the Altar or a table.

Reading: Psalm 133

O Lord our God, your servants anointed people with oil to mark as a sign of your grace. Moses anointed your holy priest Aaron to be set apart for your service in the Tabernacle and your Son Jesus was anointed by a lowly woman before his sacrifice on the cross. Bless O Lord, this oil which we now set apart a sign of your presence. Bless your servant who anoints and those who will receive anointing in this oil. Bless them to experience your wholeness of life, may you shield them from the assault of the evil one and fill them with your heavenly peace; through Jesus Christ our Lord, who lives and reigns with you and the Holy Spirit one God now and forever. **Amen.**

Minister: Let us praise the Lord

People: The Lord's name be praised

Minister: As our saviour Christ has taught us so we pray

All: **Our Father in heaven... .**

The Minister may end with the words of grace or if a presbyter is present with benediction.

130. *Operation Theatre*

Minister: Our help is in the name of the Lord.

People: **Who has made heaven and earth.**

Holy water may be sprinkled in the operation theatre.

Reading: Psalm 38

O Lord our God, you have endowed human being with wisdom and knowledge to treat serious illness with the art and skill of incision. Bless O Lord this operation theatre set up to operate and to restore health to those who suffer physical illness. Bless those who use these facilities and those who administer this place so that people may find healing and wholeness through their service; through Jesus Christ our Lord, who lives and reigns with you and the Holy Spirit one God now and forever. **Amen.**

Minister: Let us praise the Lord

People: **The Lord's name be praised**

Minister: As our saviour Christ has taught us so we pray

All: **Our Father in heaven... .**

The Minister may end with the words of grace or if a presbyter is present with benediction.

131. *Organ for Church*

Minister: Our help is in the name of the Lord.

People: **Who has made heaven and earth.**

Holy water may be sprinkled on the organ with caution.

Reading: Psalm 96.

O Lord our God, you have endowed humankind with the ability to make music to express their feelings. The musicians in the Temple in the holy of city of Jerusalem glorified your name with instruments of music. You accept the worship of your people all over world in the houses of worship as offering of praise and worship. Bless O Lord this organ and those who play this instrument of sacred music, as we set it apart for your glory so that whenever your people gather to praise you the sound of music of this organ may inspire them to worship you in Spirit and in truth; through Jesus Christ our Lord, who lives and reigns with you and the Holy Spirit one God now and forever. **Amen.**

Minister:	Let us praise the Lord
People:	**The Lord's name be praised**

Minister:	As our saviour Christ has taught us so we pray
All:	**Our Father in heaven... .**

The Minister may end with the words of grace or if a presbyter is present with benediction.

P

132. *Paramedics*

Minister:	Our help is in the name of the Lord.
People:	**Who has made heaven and earth.**

Holy water may be sprinkled on those who are gathered for blessing.

Reading: Psalm 121

O Lord our God, you heal the sick and wounded people. Your Son Jesus our Lord went about caring, treating and healing those who suffered with diseases. He assured them of forgiveness and God's compassion. Bless these your servants O Lord, that through their wisdom and skills they may bring health and wholeness to the suffering people. May the suffering people experience your healing power through their service; through Jesus Christ our Lord, who lives and reigns with you and the Holy Spirit one God now and forever. **Amen.**

Minister:	Let us praise the Lord
People:	**The Lord's name be praised**

Minister:	As our saviour Christ has taught us so we pray
All:	**Our Father in heaven... .**

The Minister may end with the words of grace or if a presbyter is present with benediction.

133. *Parliament*

Minister:	Our help is in the name of the Lord.
People:	**Who has made heaven and earth.**

Reading: Psalm 82

O Lord our God, in times past you desired that elders and prophets to advice the king in his undertakings and in the administration of governance. Bless we pray the parliament of this country with such wisdom that in all their deliberation they may protect the weak and vulnerable in society. Give them the clarity to see through the thick of complexities what is best for our country and the courage to speak and take stand for what is right; through Jesus Christ our Lord, who lives and reigns with you and the Holy Spirit one God now and forever. **Amen.**

Minister:	Let us praise the Lord
People:	**The Lord's name be praised**

Minister: As our saviour Christ has taught us so we pray

All: **Our Father in heaven... .**

The Minister may end with the words of grace or if a presbyter is present with benediction.

134.   *Parsonage*

Minister: Our help is in the name of the Lord.

People: **Who has made heaven and earth.**

Holy water may be sprinkled in the parsonage.

Reading: Psalm 34.1-15

O Lord our God, your Son Jesus lived in a house in Capernaum where people gathered in large numbers to hear his life giving word and be healed of their infirmities. Bless, this parsonage, O Lord we pray that it may be a place hallowed with prayer, and be a place of study and hospitality. May its resources be used to build up your people in faith. Bless those who live in this house with peace. Like Abraham may they welcome you in every stranger, like Elisha may they welcome foreigners and like Lazarus, Mary and Martha may they welcome you in this house. May they encourage those who are broken, and may they pray with those who need you. May their table have ample food for all to enjoy fellowship; through Jesus Christ our Lord, who lives and reigns with you and the Holy Spirit one God now and forever. **Amen.**

Minister: Let us praise the Lord

People: **The Lord's name be praised**

Minister: As our saviour Christ has taught us so we pray

All: **Our Father in heaven... .**

The Minister may end with the words of grace or if a presbyter is present with benediction.

135. *Park*

Minister: Our help is in the name of the Lord.

People: Who has made heaven and earth.

Reading: Psalm 65

O Lord our God, you made the first garden in the East for Adam and Eve to life and enjoy the harmony and beauty of nature, and you filled the heart of Joseph of Arimathea to lend the grave in his garden to bury your Son who died on the cross to save us from the snares of hell; bless this park O Lord and bless all those who work to keep it beautiful, bless all those who come here to visit for rejuvenation of their heart and mind. May it be endowed with flowers and trees, birds and animals to reflect the richness and diversity of all that you have created; through Jesus Christ our Lord, who lives and reigns with you and the Holy Spirit one God now and forever. **Amen.**

Minister: Let us praise the Lord

People: The Lord's name be praised

Minister: As our saviour Christ has taught us so we pray

All: Our Father in heaven... .

The Minister may end with the words of grace or if a presbyter is present with benediction.

136. *Pets*

Minister: Our help is in the name of the Lord.

People: Who has made heaven and earth.

Reading: Isaiah 65.17-25

O Lord our God, your grace poured out in creation and you filled the seas with fish and land with animals. Balaam's donkey saw the angel and saved his maser's life, king Solomon had many animals and birds to cherish and to study. The wise sage taught us the lesson of hard work from ants and you did not destroy Nineveh a city full of people and cattle. You gave intelligence to many of these creatures to know and love their masters. Bless O Lord this animal [these animals] that lives with us. Bless their owners, give them wisdom and strength to take care of their pets and to enjoy their company, and give good health to their animals; through Jesus Christ our Lord, who lives and reigns with you and the Holy Spirit one God now and forever. **Amen.**

Minister: Let us praise the Lord

People: The Lord's name be praised

Minister: As our saviour Christ has taught us so we pray

All: Our Father in heaven... .

The Minister may end with the words of grace or if a presbyter is present with benediction.

137.   *Perambulator (pram)*

Minister: Our help is in the name of the Lord.

People: Who has made heaven and earth.

Holy water may be sprinkled on the pram.

Reading: Psalm 117

O Lord our God, you bless each generation with children and you give us strength and wisdom to nurture them. Bless this perambulator made for infants and bless those who will use it. Keep the little ones safe and happy in it; through Jesus Christ our Lord, who lives, and reigns with you and the Holy Spirit one God now and forever. **Amen.**

Minister: Let us praise the Lord

People: The Lord's name be praised

Minister:	As our saviour Christ has taught us so we pray
All:	**Our Father in heaven... .**

The Minister may end with the words of grace or if a presbyter is present with benediction.

138. Pew

Minister:	Our help is in the name of the Lord.
People:	**Who has made heaven and earth.**

Holy water may be sprinkled on the pews.

Reading: Psalm 110

O Lord our God, you summon your people from east and west, north and south to gather to worship you. Bless these pews now installed in this house of prayer. Bless those who will gather here and use them so that they may praise you with dignity. May they hear your word attentively and celebrate your presence in sacrament joyfully; through Jesus Christ our Lord, who lives and reigns with you and the Holy Spirit one God now and forever. **Amen.**

Minister:	Let us praise the Lord
People:	**The Lord's name be praised**

Minister:	As our saviour Christ has taught us so we pray
All:	**Our Father in heaven... .**

The Minister may end with the words of grace or if a presbyter is present with benediction.

139. Piano

Minister:	Our help is in the name of the Lord.
People:	**Who has made heaven and earth.**

Holy water may be sprinkled on the piano with caution.

Reading: Psalm 150

O Lord our God, you have endowed humankind with the ability to make music to express their feelings. The musicians in the Temple in the holy of city of Jerusalem glorified your name with instruments of music. You accept the worship of your people all over world in the houses of worship as offering of praise and thanksgiving. Bless O Lord this piano and those who play it, and as we set it apart for your glory grant that whenever your people gather to praise you, the music of this instrument may inspire them to worship you in Spirit and in truth; through Jesus Christ our Lord, who lives, and reigns with you and the Holy Spirit one God now and forever. **Amen.**

Minister: Let us praise the Lord

People: The Lord's name be praised

Minister: As our saviour Christ has taught us so we pray

All: Our Father in heaven... .

The Minister may end with the words of grace or if a presbyter is present with benediction.

140. *Picture (Religious)*

Minister: Our help is in the name of the Lord.

People: Who has made heaven and earth.

Holy water may be sprinkled on the picture.

Reading: Psalm 96

O Lord our God, you endowed us with creativity to express our love for you in art. The sacred art of the artists helps us to know you and inspire us to worship you. Bless this holy picture [depicting _____ (birth, last supper, death etc. of your Son)] displayed in your honour to remind us of you and to witness our faith to others. Bless those who will see it and those who will be inspired that they may grow with us in faith and commitment to you; through Jesus Christ our Lord, who lives, and reigns with you and the Holy Spirit one God now and forever. **Amen.**

Minister:	Let us praise the Lord
People:	**The Lord's name be praised**

Minister:	As our saviour Christ has taught us so we pray
All:	**Our Father in heaven... .**

The Minister may end with the words of grace or if a presbyter is present with benediction.

141. *Plants*

Minister:	Our help is in the name of the Lord.
People:	**Who has made heaven and earth.**

Holy water may be sprinkled on the plants.

Reading: Psalm 104.14-17

O God our creator, you made all the plants of this earth. You blessed them to grow and bear fruits and flowers so that the life may be enriched with diversity. Bless this plant O Lord to be health and strong so that it may enhance life and be a source of delight to us. Bless its owner with diligence to tend it with adequate water, manure and light. We ask this through Jesus Christ our Lord, who lives, and reigns with you and the Holy Spirit one God now and forever. **Amen.**

Minister:	Let us praise the Lord
People:	**The Lord's name be praised**

Minister:	As our saviour Christ has taught us so we pray
All:	**Our Father in heaven... .**

The Minister may end with the words of grace or if a presbyter is present with benediction.

142. *Play grounds*

Minister: Our help is in the name of the Lord.

People: Who has made heaven and earth.

Holy water may be sprinkled on some part of the play ground.

Reading: Psalm 105.1-4

O Lord our God, you gave our children and young people he ability play so that they may grow adequately in their body. Bless this ground O Lord we pray which we now set apart for our children and young people to play. May they learn through games to the values of discipline, cooperation and honesty. May they develop sportsman spirit and lasting friendships; through Jesus Christ our Lord, who lives and reigns with you and the Holy Spirit one God now and forever. **Amen.**

Minister: Let us praise the Lord

People: The Lord's name be praised

Minister: As our saviour Christ has taught us so we pray

All: Our Father in heaven... .

The Minister may end with the words of grace or if a presbyter is present with benediction.

143. *Pool (swimming)*

Minister: Our help is in the name of the Lord.

People: Who has made heaven and earth.

Holy water may be sprinkled in the swimming pool.

Reading: Psalm 29.1-4

O Lord our God, you put limits to the tides of water and made fish and animals to live in it. You sent angel to shake the water of the pool of Bethzatha bringing healing to sick where your Son Jesus healed a man sick for thirty eight years. You have given us ability to swim and enjoy ourselves. Bless we pray this swimming pool as a place of sports and enjoyment. Keep those who use it safe from accidents and give wisdom to those responsible for its maintenance to be diligent in its upkeep; through Jesus Christ our Lord, who lives and reigns with you and the Holy Spirit one God now and forever. **Amen.**

Minister: Let us praise the Lord

People: **The Lord's name be praised**

Minister: As our saviour Christ has taught us so we pray

All: **Our Father in heaven... .**

The Minister may end with the words of grace or if a presbyter is present with benediction.

144.   *Prayer room*

Minister: Our help is in the name of the Lord.

People: **Who has made heaven and earth.**

Holy water may be sprinkled in the prayer room.

Reading: Psalm 121

O Lord our God, you have made us for yourself and our hearts are restless until we find our peace in you. Send forth your Holy Spirit to sanctify and bless this prayer room, O Lord so all those who come to this place to pray may find quiet and peace in your presence; through Jesus Christ our Lord, who lives and reigns with you and the Holy Spirit one God now and forever. **Amen.**

Minister: Let us praise the Lord

People: **The Lord's name be praised**

Minister: As our saviour Christ has taught us so we pray

All: **Our Father in heaven... .**

The Minister may end with the words of grace or if a presbyter is present with benediction.

145.   *Printing machine*

Minister: Our help is in the name of the Lord.

People: Who has made heaven and earth.

Holy water may be sprinkled on the printing machine.

Reading: Psalm 45.1

O Lord our God, you have given us the ability to read and write in various languages and to communicate with one another. Your Son Jesus Christ read the scriptures in Nazareth and preached his first sermon. We thank you for the scribes who with their hands wrote scriptures so that we may read it and communicate your message to others. We thank you for the development of printing technology. Now O Lord we ask your blessing this printing machine. Keep those who work to run this machine safe from all accidents and injuries. May it be a source of producing good literature; through Jesus Christ our Lord, who lives and reigns with you and the Holy Spirit one God now and forever. **Amen.**

Minister: Let us praise the Lord

People: The Lord's name be praised

Minister: As our saviour Christ has taught us so we pray

All: Our Father in heaven... .

The Minister may end with the words of grace or if a presbyter is present with benediction.

146.   *Purificator*

Minister: Our help is in the name of the Lord.

People: Who has made heaven and earth.

Holy water may be sprinkled on the purificators.

O Lord our God, bless these purificators which will used to wipe and clean the holy vessels of your sanctuary. Keep us O

Lord, pure and clean from within so that through the sacraments duly administered by your presbyters your divine life may grow in us; through Jesus Christ our Lord, who lives and reigns with you and the Holy Spirit one God now and forever. **Amen.**

Minister: Let us praise the Lord

People: **The Lord's name be praised**

Minister: As our saviour Christ has taught us so we pray

All: **Our Father in heaven... .**

The Minister may end with the words of grace or if a presbyter is present with benediction.

Q

147.   *Quilt*

Minister: Our help is in the name of the Lord.

People: **Who has made heaven and earth.**

Holy water may be sprinkled on the quilts.

Reading: Psalm 16

O Lord our God, we thank you for providing us in cotton and fleece, wool and fur to keep us warm. Bless these quilts, O Lord and all those who use them that they may sleep in warmth in this winter and be protected from diseases; through Jesus Christ our Lord, who lives and reigns with you and the Holy Spirit one God now and forever. **Amen.**

Minister: Let us praise the Lord

People: **The Lord's name be praised**

Minister: As our saviour Christ has taught us so we pray

All: **Our Father in heaven... .**

The Minister may end with the words of grace or if a presbyter is present with benediction.

R

148.   *Refectory (Dining Room)*

Minister: Our help is in the name of the Lord.

People: Who has made heaven and earth.

Holy water may be sprinkled in the Refectory or the Dining room/ hall.

Reading: Psalm 104.24-28

O Lord our God, creator of the world. In your mercy you give us the fruit of the earth and you bless us with the produce of the land. Bless O Lord, this refectory (or Dining room/hall) which we set apart for fellowship of the table. Give is grateful hearts always to thank you for your abundance, give us graciousness to welcome all people to enjoy happiness of eating together, make us generous to share whatever we have with others; through Jesus Christ our Lord, who lives and reigns with you and the Holy Spirit one God now and forever. **Amen.**

Minister: Let us praise the Lord

People: The Lord's name be praised

Minister: As our saviour Christ has taught us so we pray

All: Our Father in heaven... .

The Minister may end with the words of grace or if a presbyter is present with benediction.

149. *Refrigerator*

Minister: Our help is in the name of the Lord.

People: **Who has made heaven and earth.**

Holy water may be sprinkled in the rooms of the House with appropriate prayers. At the end this prayer may be said by the Minister or Presbyter or Bishop.

Reading: Psalm 104. 14-24

O Lord our God, you have generously provided food for us form this earth and you want us to enjoy the variety of it; bless O Lord this refrigerator to preserve food for us that all who partake of it may enjoy good health; through Jesus Christ our Lord, who lives and reigns with you and the Holy Spirit one God now and forever. **Amen.**

Minister: Let us praise the Lord

People: **The Lord's name be praised**

Minister: As our saviour Christ has taught us so we pray

All: **Our Father in heaven... .**

The Minister may end with the words of grace or if a presbyter is present with benediction.

150. *Religious House*

Minister: Our help is in the name of the Lord.

People: **Who has made heaven and earth.**

Holy water may be sprinkled in the rooms of the House with appropriate prayers. At the end this prayer may be said by the Minister or Presbyter or Bishop.

Reading: Psalm 137

O Lord our God, your people in their exile built houses and lived in Babylon till the day of their return. We ask you to bless this House which we now set apart for this Religious

Community (or _____ name of the Religious Community) so that by their discipline, worship and labours they may live in this world as those who don't belong to this world. May they glorify your name and spread the message of your love in Christ crucified to the people; through Jesus Christ our Lord, who lives and reigns with you and the Holy Spirit one God now and forever. **Amen.**

Minister:	Let us praise the Lord
People:	**The Lord's name be praised**

Minister:	As our saviour Christ has taught us so we pray
All:	**Our Father in heaven... .**

The Minister may end with the words of grace or if a presbyter is present with benediction.

151. *Restaurant*

Minister:	Our help is in the name of the Lord.
People:	**Who has made heaven and earth.**

Holy water may be sprinkled in the restaurant.

Reading: Psalm 104.24-28

O Lord our God, your Son Jesus called those who were tired to come to him and find rest; bless O Lord we beseech you this restaurant for providing rest and refreshment to those who travel and are tired that refreshed and nourish they may accomplish their tasks and reach their destiny in safety; through Jesus Christ our Lord, who lives and reigns with you and the Holy Spirit one God now and forever. **Amen.**

Minister:	Let us praise the Lord
People:	**The Lord's name be praised**

Minister:	As our saviour Christ has taught us so we pray
All:	**Our Father in heaven... .**

The Minister may end with the words of grace or if a presbyter is present with benediction.

152.   *Research Centre*

Minister: Our help is in the name of the Lord.

People: Who has made heaven and earth.

Holy water may be sprinkled in the Research Centre.

Reading: Psalm 111

O Lord our God, you have created us human being with mind and intelligence to investigate and analyse and discover the wonders of what you have created; bless O Lord this centre of research (for _____), bless those who work here that their work may flourish for the benefit of the people; through Jesus Christ our Lord, who lives and reigns with you and the Holy Spirit one God now and forever. **Amen.**

Minister: Let us praise the Lord

People: The Lord's name be praised

Minister: As our saviour Christ has taught us so we pray

All: Our Father in heaven... .

The Minister may end with the words of grace or if a presbyter is present with benediction.

153.   *Road*

Minister: Our help is in the name of the Lord.

People: Who has made heaven and earth.

Holy water may be sprinkled on some part of the road.

Reading: Psalm 122

O Lord our God, your Son Jesus travelled all over Galilee and your apostles Peter and Paul undertook international journeys to proclaim the gospel to those who were far and near; bless

O Lord this road and those who use it, keep them secure from all harm till they reach their destination in safety; through Jesus Christ our Lord, who lives and reigns with you and the Holy Spirit one God now and forever. **Amen.**

Minister: Let us praise the Lord

People: **The Lord's name be praised**

Minister: As our saviour Christ has taught us so we pray

All: **Our Father in heaven... .**

The Minister may end with the words of grace or if a presbyter is present with benediction.

S

154.   *Servers (at the Altars)*

Minister: Our help is in the name of the Lord.

People: **Who has made heaven and earth.**

Holy water may be sprinkled on the Servers or Altar boys and girls (Crucifer, Acolytes, thurifer etc).

Reading: Psalm 138

Blessed are you, O Lord our God, you appointed the tribe of Levis to serve you at the Temple in Jerusalem day and night; bless O Lord these Servers for the levitical services at the holy altar of this church; bless them with alertness, diligence and faithfulness so that the discipline of this service may form in them the strength of character; through Jesus Christ our Lord, who lives and reigns with you and the Holy Spirit one God now and forever. **Amen.**

Minister: Let us praise the Lord

People: **The Lord's name be praised**

| Minister: | As our saviour Christ has taught us so we pray |
| **All:** | **Our Father in heaven... .** |

The Minister may end with the words of grace or if a presbyter is present with benediction.

155.   *Sewing Machine*

| Minister: | Our help is in the name of the Lord. |
| **People:** | **Who has made heaven and earth.** |

Holy water may be sprinkled on some part of the road.

Reading: Psalm 117

Blessed are you, O Lord our God, for endowing your creatures with the gift and skill of craft; bless this sewing machine and those who work on it with stamina, diligence and intelligence that their endeavours may of use many; through Jesus Christ our Lord, who lives and reigns with you and the Holy Spirit one God now and forever. **Amen.**

| Minister: | Let us praise the Lord |
| **People:** | **The Lord's name be praised** |

| Minister: | As our saviour Christ has taught us so we pray |
| **All:** | **Our Father in heaven... .** |

The Minister may end with the words of grace or if a presbyter is present with benediction.

156.   *Shop*

| Minister: | Our help is in the name of the Lord. |
| **People:** | **Who has made heaven and earth.** |

Holy water may be sprinkled in the shop.

Reading: Psalm 34

Blessed are you, O Lord our God, governor of this world, you have made us human beings with insight to trade and provide for one another's need; bless O Lord this shop for the purpose it has been established that their provision may duly meets the needs of the people who live this area. Bless those who administer this shop with intelligence for commerce and skills to trade that the business may flourish and people may be benefitted; through Jesus Christ our Lord, who lives and reigns with you and the Holy Spirit one God now and forever. **Amen.**

Minister:	Let us praise the Lord
People:	**The Lord's name be praised**

Minister:	As our saviour Christ has taught us so we pray
All:	**Our Father in heaven... .**

The Minister may end with the words of grace or if a presbyter is present with benediction.

157.   *Social Service Centre*

Minister:	Our help is in the name of the Lord.
People:	**Who has made heaven and earth.**

Holy water may be sprinkled in the building or in some part of it.
Reading: Psalm 10

Blessed are you, O Lord our God, your servants and prophets told us of your concern for building communities, to empower the weak and to resist oppression; bless O Lord this Social Service Centre to enflame the hearts and minds of the people with hope that through their capability and your power they can society and make their life happy and prosperous; through Jesus Christ our Lord, who lives and reigns with you and the Holy Spirit one God now and forever. **Amen.**

Minister:	Let us praise the Lord
People:	**The Lord's name be praised**

Minister:	As our saviour Christ has taught us so we pray
All:	**Our Father in heaven... .**

The Minister may end with the words of grace or if a presbyter is present with benediction.

158. Stadium

Minister:	Our help is in the name of the Lord.
People:	**Who has made heaven and earth.**

Holy water may be sprinkled on some part of the (school) stadium.

Blessed are you, O Lord our God, you gave us physical bodies to live and enjoy the beauty of this world and your creation around us; bless this stadium O Lord we pray; may those who use it and those who coach may duly develop their physical body; may they enjoy health and vigour and may their sports and games bring enjoyment to all; through Jesus Christ our Lord, who lives and reigns with you and the Holy Spirit one God now and forever. **Amen.**

Minister:	Let us praise the Lord
People:	**The Lord's name be praised**

Minister:	As our saviour Christ has taught us so we pray
All:	**Our Father in heaven... .**

The Minister may end with the words of grace or if a presbyter is present with benediction.

159. Stage

Minister:	Our help is in the name of the Lord.
People:	**Who has made heaven and earth.**

Holy water may be sprinkled on some part of the stage.

Blessed are you, O Lord our God, you gave us the gift for performance to raise our awareness of the quality of life through the art of drama, pageant, concert, debate and public presentations; bless we O Lord we pray this stage that those who make their presentations and performances here may bring us wisdom and be a source of joy to all; through Jesus Christ our Lord, who lives and reigns with you and the Holy Spirit one God now and forever. **Amen.**

Minister:	Let us praise the Lord
People:	**The Lord's name be praised**

Minister:	As our saviour Christ has taught us so we pray
All:	**Our Father in heaven... .**

The Minister may end with the words of grace or if a presbyter is present with benediction.

160.   *Staircase*

Minister:	Our help is in the name of the Lord.
People:	**Who has made heaven and earth.**

Holy water may be sprinkled on some part of the stage.

Blessed are you, O Lord our God, your servant Jacob in his dream saw a ladder set between heaven and earth on which the angels ascended and descended; we ask your presence with us to bless this staircase; we pray O Lord that every step this staircase may be safe for people to use, that none who use it may be injured; through Jesus Christ our Lord, who lives and reigns with you and the Holy Spirit one God now and forever. **Amen.**

Minister:	Let us praise the Lord
People:	**The Lord's name be praised**

Minister: As our saviour Christ has taught us so we pray

All: **Our Father in heaven... .**

The Minister may end with the words of grace or if a presbyter is present with benediction.

161.   *Students*

Minister: Our help is in the name of the Lord.

People: **Who has made heaven and earth.**

Holy water may be sprinkled on the students.

Reading: Psalm 119.9-16

Blessed are you, O Lord our God, your servant Paul was Gamaliel's student and Mark learnt the gospel as Peter's pupil; bless O Lord these students with intellect, alertness and stamina to do well in their study and research. May they become good scholars and their insights and research bring happiness to many others; through Jesus Christ our Lord, who lives and reigns with you and the Holy Spirit one God now and forever. **Amen.**

Minister: Let us praise the Lord

People: **The Lord's name be praised**

Minister: As our saviour Christ has taught us so we pray

All: **Our Father in heaven... .**

The Minister may end with the words of grace or if a presbyter is present with benediction.

162.   *Sunday school children*

Minister: Our help is in the name of the Lord.

People: **Who has made heaven and earth.**

Holy water may be sprinkled on the Sunday school children.

Reading: Psalm 119.9-16

Blessed are you, O Lord our God, you endowed young Samuel with intelligence and purity to be Eli's student in the Holy place; bless O Lord these children enrolled in the Sunday School with such interest and enthusiasm that through the knowledge of the scriptures they may know you as their God, they may love you as their heavenly Father and they may serve you as their Lord; through Jesus Christ our Lord, who lives and reigns with you and the Holy Spirit one God now and forever. **Amen.**

Minister:	Let us praise the Lord
People:	**The Lord's name be praised**

Minister:	As our saviour Christ has taught us so we pray
All:	**Our Father in heaven... .**

The Minister may end with the words of grace or if a presbyter is present with benediction.

163. Sweets

Minister:	Our help is in the name of the Lord.
People:	**Who has made heaven and earth.**

Holy water may be sprinkled on the sweets.

Blessed are you, O Lord our God, in your goodness you made the bees to produce honey in nature; your servant Samson found honey in the carcass of the Lion, he ate it to receive strength when he was famished on his journey; bless O Lord these sweets, may it bring joy and strength to those who eat it; through Jesus Christ our Lord, who lives and reigns with you and the Holy Spirit one God now and forever. **Amen.**

Minister:	Let us praise the Lord
People:	**The Lord's name be praised**

Minister:	As our saviour Christ has taught us so we pray
All:	**Our Father in heaven... .**

The Minister may end with the words of grace or if a presbyter is present with benediction.

T

164. *Teachers*

Minister:	Our help is in the name of the Lord.
People:	**Who has made heaven and earth.**

Holy water may be sprinkled on the teachers.

Reading: Psalm 119.97-104

Blessed are you O Lord our God, in your goodness you gave the gift of Holy Spirit to your people and appointed teachers and people with diverse gifts to build up the community life of the believers; bless O Lord these your servants who have offered their lives to teach; give them stamina, wisdom and commitment to not only to teach but to impart strength of character to their pupils; through Jesus Christ our Lord, who lives and reigns with you and the Holy Spirit one God now and forever. **Amen.**

Minister:	Let us praise the Lord
People:	**The Lord's name be praised**

Minister:	As our saviour Christ has taught us so we pray
All:	**Our Father in heaven... .**

The Minister may end with the words of grace or if a presbyter is present with benediction.

165. *Television Set*

Minister: Our help is in the name of the Lord.

People: Who has made heaven and earth.

Blessed are you O Lord our God, you have blessed us with eyes to see and ears to hear; bless O Lord this television set for the benefit of your servants that they may see and hear all that is useful for their knowledge and recreation; through Jesus Christ our Lord, who lives and reigns with you and the Holy Spirit one God now and forever. **Amen.**

Minister: Let us praise the Lord

People: The Lord's name be praised

Minister: As our saviour Christ has taught us so we pray

All: Our Father in heaven... .

The Minister may end with the words of grace or if a presbyter is present with benediction.

166. *Tower (Church)*

Minister: Our help is in the name of the Lord.

People: Who has made heaven and earth.

Holy water may be sprinkled in the tower.

Reading: Psalm 61

Blessed are you O Lord our God, your Son over came the temptation of the tempter at the pinnacle of the Temple; Bless O Lord this tower, the pinnacle of this (Church) building, with strength and safety that it be a landmark in this area, and the sound of bells from there may go forth everywhere calling the faithful to prayer and reminding all others of your ever abiding presence among your people; through Jesus Christ our Lord, who lives and reigns with you and the Holy Spirit one God now and forever. **Amen.**

Minister:	Let us praise the Lord
People:	**The Lord's name be praised**

Minister:	As our saviour Christ has taught us so we pray
All:	**Our Father in heaven... .**

The Minister may end with the words of grace or if a presbyter is present with benediction.

167. *Tractor*

Minister:	Our help is in the name of the Lord.
People:	**Who has made heaven and earth.**

Holy water may be sprinkled on the tractor to bless it.

Reading: Psalm 8

Blessed are you O Lord our God, in your goodness you gave the gift and aptitude to cultivate crops; bless O Lord this tractor now to be used for the cultivating fields, bless your servant who will use it with stamina and diligence so that they may enjoy the rich harvest of crops; through Jesus Christ our Lord, who lives and reigns with you and the Holy Spirit one God now and forever. **Amen.**

Minister:	Let us praise the Lord
People:	**The Lord's name be praised**

Minister:	As our saviour Christ has taught us so we pray
All:	**Our Father in heaven... .**

The Minister may end with the words of grace or if a presbyter is present with benediction.

168.   *Training Centre*

Minister: Our help is in the name of the Lord.

People: Who has made heaven and earth.

Holy water may be sprinkled in the training centre.

Blessed are you O Lord our God, only through the aid of your Spirit people learn the skill of vocation and develop intellectual quality of life; Bless, O Lord, this training Centre and all those who use it, keep it safe and secure from all harm and accidents and may those who instruct and those who are trained alike may be of good use to bring happiness to others through their skills and learning; through Jesus Christ our Lord, who lives and reigns with you and the Holy Spirit one God now and forever. **Amen.**

Minister: Let us praise the Lord

People: The Lord's name be praised

Minister: As our saviour Christ has taught us so we pray

All: Our Father in heaven... .

The Minister may end with the words of grace or if a presbyter is present with benediction.

169.   *Trees*

Minister: Our help is in the name of the Lord.

People: Who has made heaven and earth.

Holy water may be on the tree.

Reading: Psalm 1

Blessed are you O Lord our God, in your goodness you created the all sorts of trees to bring health, healing and delight to human beings; Bless this tree/*these trees*, with healthy life, proper growth and length of years that it may sustain variety of birds and animals, insects and worms in it, and may remind us of the tree of life with its healing leaves and perpetual yield of fruit in the new earth; through Jesus Christ our Lord, who lives and reigns with you and the Holy Spirit one God now and forever. **Amen.**

Minister:	Let us praise the Lord
People:	**The Lord's name be praised**

Minister:	As our saviour Christ has taught us so we pray
All:	**Our Father in heaven... .**

The Minister may end with the words of grace or if a presbyter is present with benediction.

u

170. *University*

Minister:	Our help is in the name of the Lord.
People:	**Who has made heaven and earth.**

Reading: Psalm 19

Blessed are you O Lord our God, in your goodness you commanded Moses to teach the Law to your people; Bless O Lord we beseech you this university that in it may knowledge and sound learning may flourish and abound, inspire all those who teach and all who learn, and grant that in humility of heart they may always look to you, the fountain of all wisdom; through Jesus Christ our Lord, who lives and reigns with you and the Holy Spirit one God now and forever. **Amen.**

Minister:	Let us praise the Lord
People:	**The Lord's name be praised**

Minister:	As our saviour Christ has taught us so we pray
All:	**Our Father in heaven... .**

The Minister may end with the words of grace or if a presbyter is present with benediction.

171.   *Utensils*

Minister: Our help is in the name of the Lord.

People: Who has made heaven and earth.

Holy water may be sprinkled on the utensils.

Blessed are you O Lord our God, in your goodness you dined with Abraham and blessed him; We beseech you O Lord to bless these utensils for cooking and those who will use them, that the food prepared in them may be a source of nourishment for health, strength and happiness to all; through Jesus Christ our Lord, who lives and reigns with you and the Holy Spirit one God now and forever. **Amen.**

Minister: Let us praise the Lord

People: The Lord's name be praised

Minister: As our saviour Christ has taught us so we pray

All: Our Father in heaven... .

The Minister may end with the words of grace or if a presbyter is present with benediction.

172.   *Uniforms*

Minister: Our help is in the name of the Lord.

People: Who has made heaven and earth.

Holy water may be sprinkled on the uniforms.

Blessed are you O Lord our God, in your goodness you gave the priests and levites vestments to serve in your Tabernacle; Bless O Lord these uniforms now ready for use and clothe those who use them with a sense of self worth for what they undertake to do as their responsibility, let those who they serve may regard them with due dignity; through Jesus Christ our Lord, who lives and reigns with you and the Holy Spirit one God now and forever. **Amen.**

Minister:	Let us praise the Lord
People:	**The Lord's name be praised**

Minister:	As our saviour Christ has taught us so we pray
All:	**Our Father in heaven... .**

The Minister may end with the words of grace or if a presbyter is present with benediction.

V

173. *Vehicles*

Minister:	Our help is in the name of the Lord.
People:	**Who has made heaven and earth.**

Holy water may be sprinkled on the vehicle.

Read Psalm 66.1-6

Blessed are you O Lord our God, in your goodness you created this world and implanted in us interest to travel and curiosity to explore; bless O Lord our God this vehicle (*car, motorcycle, scooter etc*) and bless also your servant who use it that they may in safety accomplish their good purpose; through Jesus Christ our Lord, who lives and reigns with you and the Holy Spirit one God now and forever. **Amen.**

Minister:	Let us praise the Lord
People:	**The Lord's name be praised**

Minister:	As our saviour Christ has taught us so we pray
All:	**Our Father in heaven... .**

The Minister may end with the words of grace or if a presbyter is present with benediction.

174.   Vegetables

Minister: Our help is in the name of the Lord.

People: Who has made heaven and earth.

Holy water may be sprinkled on the vegetables.

Reading: Psalm 104.1 & 10-16

Blessed are you O Lord our God, in your goodness you created all kinds of seed giving plants and vegetables for use of human beings; you blessed them to multiply and fill the earth; Bless O Lord these vegetables to flourish with good growth so that it may be a source of good nourishment and health to the people; through Jesus Christ our Lord, who lives and reigns with you and the Holy Spirit one God now and forever. **Amen.**

Minister: Let us praise the Lord

People: The Lord's name be praised

Minister: As our saviour Christ has taught us so we pray

All: Our Father in heaven... .

The Minister may end with the words of grace or if a presbyter is present with benediction.

175.   Vessels (Holy)

Minister: Our help is in the name of the Lord.

People: Who has made heaven and earth.

Holy water may be sprinkled on the uniforms.

Reading: Psalm 65.1-4

Blessed are you O Lord our God, in your goodness you gave us the gift of Holy Eucharist as a sign and a means of your grace and favour to us; Bless O Lord these holy vessels now set apart for sacred use of celebrating the great mystery of our faith and bless the your Ministers with faith, dignity and reverence for you; through Jesus Christ our Lord, who lives and reigns with you and the Holy Spirit one God now and forever. **Amen.**

Minister:	Let us praise the Lord
People:	**The Lord's name be praised**

Minister:	As our saviour Christ has taught us so we pray
All:	**Our Father in heaven... .**

The Minister may end with the words of grace or if a presbyter is present with benediction.

176. *Veterinary Centre*

Minister:	Our help is in the name of the Lord.
People:	**Who has made heaven and earth.**

Holy water may be sprinkled in the Veterinary Centre.

Reading: Psalm 104.1 & 14-24

Blessed are you O Lord our God, in your goodness you created all kinds of animals to bring forth after their kinds; you made the donkey to speak and save Balaam from perishing from the hands of angel, you sent ravens to being bread for your prophet Elijah to save his life; Bless O Lord we beseech you this centre set up to provide treatment to animals for their illnesses, bless the doctors and their helpers that the animals cured and strengthened by work filled with harness of strength; through Jesus Christ our Lord, who lives and reigns with you and the Holy Spirit one God now and forever. **Amen.**

Minister:	Let us praise the Lord
People:	**The Lord's name be praised**

Minister: As our saviour Christ has taught us so we pray

All: Our Father in heaven... .

The Minister may end with the words of grace or if a presbyter is present with benediction.

177.   *Vestments*

Minister: Our help is in the name of the Lord.

People: Who has made heaven and earth.

Holy water may be sprinkled on the uniforms.

Blessed are you O Lord our God, in your goodness you instructed your servant Moses to provide beautiful vestments for Aaron and all priests to serve before you in your Holy Tabernacle; bless O Lord our God these vestment now set apart for the sacred use of your priests to minister your people with word and sacraments; through Jesus Christ our Lord, who lives and reigns with you and the Holy Spirit one God now and forever. **Amen.**

Minister: Let us praise the Lord

People: The Lord's name be praised

Minister: As our saviour Christ has taught us so we pray

All: Our Father in heaven... .

The Minister may end with the words of grace or if a presbyter is present with benediction.

178.   *Vestry*

Minister: Our help is in the name of the Lord.

People: Who has made heaven and earth.

Holy water may be sprinkled in the vestry.

Reading: Psalm 15

Blessed are you O Lord our God, in you showed in vision to Ezekiel a great vision of a splendid Temple complete with Holy of Holies, altar, magnificent courts and vestibules for the use of your priests and for the glory of your name; Bless O Lord this vestry now set apart for the use of the Ministers of this Church, that it may be safe and secure to preserve vestments, documents, records and books. May this place be hallowed with prayers-of-preparations, order and discipline; through Jesus Christ our Lord, who lives and reigns with you and the Holy Spirit one God now and forever. **Amen.**

Minister: Let us praise the Lord

People: **The Lord's name be praised**

Minister: As our saviour Christ has taught us so we pray

All: **Our Father in heaven... .**

The Minister may end with the words of grace or if a presbyter is present with benediction.

W

179. *Wall*

Minister: Our help is in the name of the Lord.

People: **Who has made heaven and earth.**

Holy water may be sprinkled on the uniforms.

Reading: Psalm 147

O Lord our God, you set boundaries for seas and lands and you commanded your servant Joshua to mark the boundaries for the territories of the twelve tribes of Israel. Your Nehemiah inspired your people to gather together to rebuild the walls of the holy city of Jerusalem to make it strong and safe; Bless O Lord this wall to be the strength and safety of all those who dwell within it; through Jesus Christ our Lord, who lives and

reigns with you and the Holy Spirit one God now and forever.
Amen.

Minister: Let us praise the Lord
People: The Lord's name be praised

Minister: As our saviour Christ has taught us so we pray
All: Our Father in heaven... .

*The Minister may end with the words of grace or if a presbyter is
present with benediction.*

180.   *Ward*

Minister: Our help is in the name of the Lord.
People: Who has made heaven and earth.

Holy water may be sprinkled on the uniforms.

Reading: Psalm 134

O Lord our God, you desire that your people may dwell secure
and lie down to sleep with peaceful mind; bless O Lord we
beseech you this ward; bless those who administer it and live
in it, keep them safe and secure all harm, bless them with peace
of mind and heart; through Jesus Christ our Lord, who lives
and reigns with you and the Holy Spirit one God now and
forever. **Amen.**

Minister: Let us praise the Lord
People: The Lord's name be praised

Minister: As our saviour Christ has taught us so we pray
All: Our Father in heaven... .

*The Minister may end with the words of grace or if a presbyter is
present with benediction.*

181. *Watch*

Minister: Our help is in the name of the Lord.

People: **Who has made heaven and earth.**

Reading: Psalm 34.1-10

Blessed are you O Lord our God, you determine time and movement of Sun and planets, you have given us the ability to measure time; bless O Lord this watch and _____ (*name of the owner*) to use it for efficiently planning his/her tasks and to accomplish it with precision. May this watch enable him/her to fulfil his/her commitment to do his/her work in time; through Jesus Christ our Lord, who lives and reigns with you and the Holy Spirit one God now and forever. **Amen.**

Minister: Let us praise the Lord

People: **The Lord's name be praised**

Minister: As our saviour Christ has taught us so we pray

All: **Our Father in heaven... .**

The Minister may end with the words of grace or if a presbyter is present with benediction.

182. *Wedding anniversary*

Minister: Our help is in the name of the Lord.

People: **Who has made heaven and earth.**

Holy water may be sprinkled on the uniforms.

Reading: Psalm 23

Blessed are you O Lord our maker, you created Adam and Eve to live as husband and wife in love and mutual commitment in the garden of Eden; you surround every family with your generous love; bless O Lord our God *A* and *B* with love and patience, health and happiness; that they may be blessed with length of days and happiness of one another's companionship; through Jesus Christ our Lord, who lives and reigns with you and the Holy Spirit one God now and forever. **Amen.**

Minister: Let us praise the Lord

People: The Lord's name be praised

Minister: As our saviour Christ has taught us so we pray

All: Our Father in heaven... .

The Minister may end with the words of grace or if a presbyter is present with benediction.

183.   *Wedding cake*

Minister: Our help is in the name of the Lord.

People: Who has made heaven and earth.

Reading: Psalm 128

Blessed are you O Lord our maker, you blessed Abraham and Sarah with length of days and they flourished in health and wealth; You gave wisdom the Abraham's servant to get Rebecca to be Isaac's wife and blessed them; We beseech you to bless this wedding cake, a symbol and source of happiness to *A* and *B* and all their relatives and friends that their happiness may last all the days of their life; through Jesus Christ our Lord, who lives and reigns with you and the Holy Spirit one God now and forever. **Amen.**

Minister: Let us praise the Lord

People: The Lord's name be praised

Minister: As our saviour Christ has taught us so we pray

All: Our Father in heaven... .

The Minister may end with the words of grace or if a presbyter is present with benediction.

184.   *Well [bore or tube well]*

Minister: Our help is in the name of the Lord.

People: Who has made heaven and earth.

Holy water may be sprinkled on the well.

Reading: Psalm 23

Blessed are you O Lord our God, your Son Jesus waited at Jacob's well to quench his thirst, and he offered living water to the Samaritan woman who came to fetch water; Bless O Lord this well with abundance of freshness and sweetness to quench the thirst of people and give life to plants and trees, birds and animals; bless it to increase ecological richness here so that life may flourish in variety and in diversity; through Jesus Christ our Lord, who lives and reigns with you and the Holy Spirit one God now and forever. **Amen.**

Minister: Let us praise the Lord

People: The Lord's name be praised

Minister: As our saviour Christ has taught us so we pray

All: Our Father in heaven... .

The Minister may end with the words of grace or if a presbyter is present with benediction.

X

185.   *X-Ray Machine*

Minister: Our help is in the name of the Lord.

People: Who has made heaven and earth.

Reading: Psalm 139

Blessed are you O Lord our maker; you know our body and you give us intelligence to help all those who treat us and look after us; bless this X-ray machine and its operators that through the services of machine the sick may receive right treatment and receive health and wholeness; through Jesus Christ our Lord, who lives and reigns with you and the Holy Spirit one God now and forever. **Amen.**

Minister:	Let us praise the Lord
People:	**The Lord's name be praised**
Minister:	As our saviour Christ has taught us so we pray
All:	**Our Father in heaven… .**

The Minister may end with the words of grace or if a presbyter is present with benediction.